Ace in the Picture

Jude Tresswell

First published 2019
by Rowanvale Books Ltd
The Gate
Keppoch Street
Roath
Cardiff
CF24 3JW
www.rowanvalebooks.com

A CIP catalogue record for this book is available from the British Library.
ISBN: 978-1-912655-18-2

Chapter 1

Raith stood in the kitchen in front of the calendar. His gaze shifted from the naked figure depicted on 'October' to the highlighted 'Thursday 12th' and back again. He pressed a fingertip to his lips, transferred a kiss to the mid-point of the figure's shoulder blades and ran his finger down the spine—Mike Angells' spine.

The real-life Mike walked into the room and filled the kettle.

"What are you admirin'?" he asked. "The model or the artist?"

Raith *was* the artist. "The artist," he replied. "He's classy. The model's okay, I suppose."

"Cheeky!" Mike admonished.

Changing the subject, Raith asked, "You know what day it is in two days' time, don't you?"

"In two days? Well, let's see... difficult one... It must be Thursday. Aye, that's right. It was Monday yesterday, so—"

"Stop teasing me! Do you think he's forgotten?"

'He' was Phil Roberts, the man Raith had married 364 days earlier.

"Don't be daft. Of course not. You know Phil. His middle name's 'No fuss'."

"That's two names."

"And that's two cups of coffee. One for you. One for me," said Mike, handing over a mug.

"Here. You can have the one with the penis handle, seein' as you made it."

"None for me?" asked a third man who, yawning, had entered the kitchen. He hugged the two men already there.

"Sorry, Ross," Mike apologised. "I didn't make you one. I thought you were still asleep."

"No. Just dozy," said Ross, Mike's civil partner, sleepily. "I heard Phil's car. Is it an emergency, Raith?"

"Not exactly," Raith replied. "He went in early to cover for a colleague."

Phil had helped to pioneer a form of rectal surgery that used nanocarbon patches to reconstruct torn tissue. He was a respected consultant at the hospital an hour's drive away in Warbridge, County Durham.

"I'd better get sorted and get out myself," said Ross. He was, amongst other things, a gallery proprietor in Gateshead, and his journey to work took longer than Phil's. He yawned again.

"Are you feelin' okay?" asked Mike, alert to Ross's tone of voice. "It's not like you to sound so unenthusiastic about work." In fact, it wasn't like Ross to sound unenthusiastic about anything. He was always lively—he personified keenness.

"I'm dead tired cos I didn't sleep well. I had a strange text late on. You were already asleep. I don't think you heard the phone buzz. Strange. Unsettling."

"Oh?"

"How do you mean?" asked Raith. "We're not going to get involved with more criminal activities, are we? I'd had enough of crime fighting last time!"

Even though Mike was no longer a detective with the Tees, Tyne and Wear Constabulary, the four of them were involved in a surprising amount of crime fighting. 'Last time' had involved an illegal immigrant, and the tensions that had arisen had threatened the survival of the quad.

That's what they were: a gay, polyamorous quad. They lived in Tunhead, a hamlet in Weardale in the Durham hills. Once, Tunhead had rung to the sound of workers' hammers hitting stone. In a way it still did: Ross had turned it into an arts centre full of smiths, sculptors and potters who wanted to escape the North East's towns.

"Well, we're not, are we?" Raith repeated.

"No."

"Good. Well, my creations won't create themselves. I'd better get off, too."

In Raith's case, 'getting off' simply meant walking twenty yards to his studio, a converted storehouse.

"You sure he hasn't forgotten?" he asked Mike again before he left.

"I'm sure."

"Okay then."

"What's that about?" asked Ross after Raith was gone.

"He's bothered that Phil's forgotten their anniversary."

"He hasn't."

"I know he hasn't. He's takin' him off on a trip sumwhere—he's not sayin' where yet—but you know Raith. He needs everythin' crystal clear and written in capital letters. And sumtimes, so do I. What was this message about?"

Ross pulled a face and explained. When he'd done so, Mike could understand his concern.

"He wouldn't be so stupid, Ross… Would he?"

"Not stupid, Mike, but he's gullible. He doesn't always think. I just don't know."

* * *

The message stayed in Ross's mind during the forty-mile drive to the gallery and he couldn't forget about it once he was there. Some of Raith's paintings hung on the gallery walls. They were mainly of Weardale's waterfalls. After heavy rain, the falls transformed from gentle trickles into rushing, gushing powerful forces of nature that the four men knew could kill. They'd seen them kill.

Raith loved to paint the waterfalls. From a distance, his torrents looked alive. The effect was linked to his use of colour. Raith was a tetrachromat; he could see a host of hues in what, to most people, was a single shade. He painted for himself, though, not for fame or money—he had plenty of both, due to his skill with clay not brushes. Several of his wares were on show at the gallery, most tagged 'sold' with a price that would feed and clothe all four men for a long, long time. His sensually erotic sculptures, modelled on Mike and Phil, were always in demand and beautifully, lovingly executed. But today, Ross gave Raith's erotica a miss. He stared, instead, at the waterfalls.

What might induce Raith to produce a piece of work "with intent to deceive", as the legal phrase was?

That was what the worrying message had suggested. That Raith's were the hands and eyes behind a painting that the police were interested in. They thought it was a fake. For the umpteenth time, Ross asked himself *why?*

Raith didn't need fame and he didn't need fortune, but did he need the challenge of outwitting the experts? Of copying another artist's work so accurately that no one would notice the difference?

Surely not. Momentarily, Ross's dark mood lifted. The only challenge Raith was likely to rise to was the one of finding ways to spice up the quad's evening meals. Two nights ago, he'd 'accidentally' stumbled near the saucepan with a teaspoon of chilli flakes in his hand.

"Oh, look! They've fallen in," he'd said apologetically.

Ross smiled when he thought about it, but anxiety soon returned. Could Raith be feeling resentment? Sometimes, that was the driving force behind a fraud. Failed artists whose work had been refused once too often. Failed artists who took *I'll show them!* literally.

No. All Raith's resentments were little ones that quickly blew over—feeling nagged for not doing his turn on the house-keeping rota, being yelled at for leaving clay-covered dirty washing on top of the pile of clean laundry. Raith took umbrage easily, but he'd be smiling again within the hour. And anyway, he wasn't a failed artist. He was a very successful one.

He was a strange mixture though. That complexity was part of his attraction. It was part of what made him Raith. His skill was undeniable, but his mental health was fragile— 'bloody unhinged' was how Mike would describe Raith in less charitable moments. He could be unpredictable. He could be very violent. He had another side, though, and it was what Mike and Phil and Ross adored about him. Canny, clued up, an ex-con hard as nails... but at the toss of a coin, as loving, as sweet and as trusting as anyone they had ever met. Mike was as loving, and often as sweet, but trusting? No. Mike was ex-CID. It wasn't in his nature to be trusting.

Which was why Mike was already making phone calls.

Chapter 2

Phil sat in his Fourtrak in the hospital car park, ready to drive home. The past year had been a good one. He loved being part of the quad. Serious, reserved and a loner by nature, he'd found acceptance, affection and security with his three men, and he had as much sex as he wanted. With two of them anyway. Ross only partnered Mike.

When, early in the previous year, Phil had felt assailed by problems, he'd reacted to the strain by accusing Ross and Mike of bias and unfairness, of unbalancing the dynamics of the quad. But when he'd married Raith, the balance had been restored. In two days' time, it would be his and Raith's first wedding anniversary.

He texted his colleague: *The ops went smoothly. Thanks for swapping theatre dates.* Phil's ops had originally been scheduled for the following day, but now he could pack in the morning and fly off later in the afternoon instead. A week-long trip to Venezuela and the Angel Falls. Then, after he and Raith returned, he would still have three weeks off to laze around Tunhead and enjoy the autumn weather on the moors above the village.

He smiled as he placed the travel documents in the inside pocket of his jacket. He'd kept them at work, well out of sight.

Raith was well-travelled. He'd seen the Angel Falls four years previously, but only briefly. He'd often said how much he'd like to return and paint the rainbows made by the tumbling water.

Raith and his waterfalls! thought Phil. Well, he'd take him there, to the highest cascade in the world. Tomorrow.

Phil rounded the final bend of the narrow, twisty lane that led from Tunhope on the trunk road to their home at the head of Tun Beck. He was a little surprised to see a blue and yellow police car parked on the tarmac in front of Raith's studio, but it probably belonged to Clive Flaxby. Flaxby had been Mike's superintendent when Mike was in the Force. He sometimes visited but, being CID, usually in an unmarked car.

As soon as Phil stepped out of his Fourtrak, he realised he was mistaken. What the hell was going on?

The studio doors were open. Phil ran in and nearly bumped into a uniformed constable who was carrying a laptop out. Raith, furious, tore out after him.

"Bring that fucking laptop back, you fucking bastard!"

Raith grabbed hold of the constable's arm, then found his own restrained by a plain-clothes cop.

"You bust my fucking arm and I'll fucking kill you!" he screamed. "I'll break your fucking neck!"

Then he saw Phil, and Phil saw Mike. Mike made a gesture of helplessness. Phil went straight to Raith and, in front of everybody, put both arms tightly round the trembling man.

"Shhh now."

Raith relaxed and the DC released him from the armlock.

"Phil, what's going on?" asked Raith, still distraught but visibly calmer now the one man who *could* calm him was there, holding him tightly.

Mike, standing near the back, breathed a sigh of relief. Phil had arrived just in time. Mike had been working in the garden when the cars had pulled up outside the studio. He'd recognised the driver of the marked car. He'd recognised the knock on the studio door, too. Peremptory. No nonsense. Business. He'd put down his tools and quickly crossed the little lane—in time to hear a plain-clothes cop he didn't recognise tell Raith that they'd like him to visit the station tomorrow to answer some questions to aid an investigation, and they'd need to confiscate his PCs and phones. Raith had gone ballistic.

With the quad's patience and support, Raith had learnt to control the angry outbursts that, years ago, had seen him jailed for GBH, but rage was never far beneath his surface. When Raith erupted, the only person who could contain his wrath was Phil. Somehow, Phil could calm him and make him feel safe.

Raith let himself be held and, bewildered, repeated his question: "Phil, what's going on?"

* * *

The men were unable to discuss the day's events together until the evening, when Ross returned from work. They gathered in Cromarty's comfortable living room to talk.

Cromarty: it was the name of their home. Mike had been the first of them to move to Tunhead, many years before. He'd met Ross and—tickled by the link between Ross and Cromarty, two adjacent Scottish counties—had named the house "Cromarty" when Ross moved in.

Originally, most of the houses in the hamlet had been the homes of quarry workers, but they'd become holiday lets by that time. As few people wished to spend their holidays in this beautiful but wet, cold and remote part of North East England, the owners had been glad to sell their properties to Ross and Mike. The two of them had renovated everything in their spare time. Ross, versed in many aspects of the art and craft world, had started up the Beck on the Wear Arts Centre (known, with amusement, as BOTWAC) and leased the buildings to artisans. Raith was one. He'd long known Ross, and Mike had long known Phil.

Now, the four men lived together, having made Cromarty and the house next door into a single, much-loved home.

Ross took Mike to one side. "Keep it light, love. I know you. When it's cloak and dagger stuff, all your old police gravitas takes over, and I understand that, but..."

"You mean I can tease him?"

"You usually do."

"Aye, I know. You try to look less worried, though."

Ross pulled a face. "I can't help it," he admitted. "I know I never have sex with him—it's not that sort of love—but I do love him. Very much. And I *am* worried. For him. He's always on the edge. You know what I mean. I'm not even sure that Phil can keep him in one piece this time. Mentally, I mean."

"He worked his usual magic earlier on. But yes, I'll keep it light."

* * *

"I've got to go into Warbridge station tomorrow for a 'voluntary interview'," Raith said bitterly. "I could've answered all their fucking questions here. They don't have to drag me off to fucking Warbridge. I mean, they're not charging me with anything. It's all this stupid 'helping with enquiries' shit, and they wouldn't tell me what the fucking enquiries I'm supposed to be helping with actually are. Fucking shiters. I felt like I was eighteen years old again. Standing in the dock with some poncy, stuck-up magistrate telling me what a naughty boy I was..." Resentment gave way to fear, his brown eyes suddenly filling with concern. "I've done nothing wrong. Honestly, I haven't. I would never risk losing this, losing Phil, losing you two, and I don't want to go back to jail. If I'm going to get fucked, I want to be fucked by you and Mike," he said, turning to Phil, "not by some spiced-up, HIV-infected bastard in a jail."

All Phil could do was hold him more tightly.

"We found a few things out," said Mike. "I phoned Flaxby this mornin'— actually, before they all came."

"Before?"

"It was sumthin' Ross said."

"I'd had a text," said Ross, and he explained what had happened. "You'd already left for work, Phil."

"So, I phoned Flaxby," said Mike, "to see if anythin' had come his way. I could tell he was bein' evasive, but there was nuthin' I could do. I didn't realise things would move so fast. He phoned me later this afternoon and apologised. He knew what was happenin', but because the four of us are together, he had to keep schtum. When I say he knew what was happenin', I mean he knew that there'd be officers comin' here. That's all. He's got nuthin' to do with the actual case.

"It's not local. It's a London crew. They came up to HQ in Tyneside the other day, then turned up at the Warbridge station wantin' an office. They're a branch of the National Crime Agency. Accordin' to Flaxby, the ICU—the International Corruption Unit."

"International corruption? What on earth do they think is going on here?" asked Ross in disbelief.

"Wish I knew. The ICU remit is cybercrime, gun runnin', drugs, money launderin'. Those sorts of things. I'm assumin' this is some kind of fraud, maybe linked to money launderin'. All Flaxby could tell me was that it's sumthin' to do with Raith bein' a tetrachromat. So, I phoned Ross."

"And I've been making calls all day," Ross cut in. "In a nutshell, a painting has just been offered to a London auction house, Lenfitte's, privately. They're a Mayfair art and antiques auctioneers. Lenfitte's staff became suspicious. They don't believe the painting is authentic. The artist is supposedly a Russian woman, Masha Ivashova. She was more or less unheard of until recently, then *bang!* Lenfitte's sold two of her works for a hundred and ten thousand euros six months ago. Then this turns up. Red alert in the art world. Alarm bells ringing. Here, look."

"A hundred and ten each?" asked Phil when Ross passed his laptop over and he and Raith studied the screen.

"Yes."

"Phew!"

Mike, all cop for a moment, watched Raith carefully, and smiled to himself. Raith had been telling them the truth.

"It's like the kind of thing… oh shit," said Phil as he saw the picture, too. It was a painting that was executed in exactly the same style as Raith's, and it was a waterfall.

"What's so special about it?" Raith asked. "It looks normal to me."

"Well, it would look normal to you, but it doesn't look normal to the rest of us. It looks wrong. It's… too blue, too green. Too something."

"It's too detailed for one thing," said Ross. "In terms of the palette. I spoke with Melissa Cayson. She's the conservator who texted me—we worked at the gallery in Durham together years ago, and now she works for the auctioneers. If we had the painting here, instead of on a laptop, it would look like yours, Raith. At least, it would if it were magnified. That bubble there…" He pointed. "That wouldn't be one blue. It'd be fifty tiny, different blues. That's why it takes you so long to complete anything. You spend half your time mixing paints."

"It's a good job we depend on his ceramics to pay the bills then, isn't it?" said Mike. "We'd be gettin' final payment letters all the time."

Raith smiled for the first time that evening. He was pleased to have his contribution to the finances recognised, albeit in jest.

"So, your friend thinks it's a fake," he said, "but why point the finger at me? There must be other people who paint like that."

"No," said Ross. "That's the problem. As far as I know, there's only Masha Ivashova—and she's dead—and one other female artist. Most known artists are men, and I'm pretty sure that all the people who've tried to fake art are. It's been men historically. It's men now."

"So…?"

"So, the chances are that whoever faked this is a man, but people who see the variety and intensity of colour *you* see are usually women. Tetrachromats aren't men. At least, they shouldn't be."

"Don't talk daft, Ross. I'm a man. At least, I was last time I looked."

"Phil, you know what I mean, don't you?"

"Ross is right, love. Tetrachromatic vision is associated with women, but the research suggests that, occasionally, men can have it too. It's unusual for women to have it. It's very rare indeed for men."

"But that's why the cops are investigating you, Raith. The fraudster is likely to be male, but, unusually, he'll be a tetrachromat. Two and two make you."

Raith nodded. "I see. I suppose I'd rather be unusual than average. I like having rarity value. You will come with me tomorrow, won't you, Mike?" he asked. "You know your way around these voluntary interview things."

"Of course I will," Mike said with all the encouragement he could muster.

"I'm shattered," said Ross, glancing at the clock. "Let's leave *this* 'til tomorrow and get some rest and sleep on it. There's nothing more we can do tonight. Come here."

Phil stood up to meet his goodnight hug, as did Raith. Ross held Raith at arms' length.

"You're not in this alone," he said. "We're in it together, as always, and we'll sort it out together, as always, and everything will be fine."

Raith nodded again. "As always," he said. He trusted Ross completely.

"I'll just rinse the cups and I'll be up," said Mike, before hugging Raith and Phil too.

"'Til morning," said Phil as he gently pushed Raith in the direction of the stairs.

On the way, he passed his jacket hanging on the clothes rack by the front door. The travel tickets were burning a hole in the pocket. One thing was certain: he wouldn't be visiting Venezuela any time soon. He just hoped he wouldn't be visiting Raith in a prison cell instead.

No, as Ross had promised, everything would be fine.

Chapter 3

All four men were glad it was October. They weren't woken by birdsong or an early sunrise. It was nine o'clock when Mike came downstairs and found Ross already on his mobile.

"I'm contacting everyone I know to see if other Ivashovas have turned up recently," he explained.

"You're not goin' into work then?"

"No. I'm sure they can manage without me for a day or two."

Phil and Raith came into the living room and overheard.

"I'm not in today, either," said Phil. He didn't tell Raith he'd already planned to be absent. "What can I do? Any ideas?"

"Yes," said Mike. "Print out anythin' and everythin' that's on the web about this painter, Masha Ivashova. Don't just download it. Hard copies."

Phil nodded meekly. He'd learnt a harsh lesson the previous year. When Mike was in detective mode, it was sensible to do exactly what he said, even though he was no longer in the Force.

"What are you going to do?" he asked as he sat down.

"Contact Flaxby to try and get more background before I go to the VI with Raith. What have they got on him, other than the fact that they think he's got tetrachromatic vision?"

"What about me?" asked Raith. "What can I do?"

"Make the tea," said Mike.

Raith looked hurt. Ross and Phil looked furious. As soon as he'd said it, Mike wished he hadn't. "Shit, I'm sorry," he said apologetically.

'I'm sorry' didn't go down too well with Raith. "Is that how you used to talk to your underlings when you were at the station?" he asked.

"No. I'm sorry," Mike repeated. "Really. I'm sorry."

But what *could* Raith do? No point asking him to make any written notes about this Masha woman. She'd have died in 1491 instead of 1941. He had an idea. MO: *modus operandi*.

"Raith, can you use the clearest PC screen we've got and study this waterfall picture?"

"Why? What am I looking for?"

"You might see sumthin' that strikes you as different from your normal way of executin' things."

"We'd need an original painting, Mike," said Ross. "The more Raith zooms in on screen, the fuzzier it'll go." Mike kicked his ankle gently. He took the hint. "It's a starting point, though," Ross said encouragingly. "You might notice something."

"Could we get hold of the original?" asked Phil. "The one the fuss is about? Would it be at the auction house?"

"No. Fraud squad will have taken it," said Mike. "They'll have it safely locked up sumwhere in London. At least, I reckon so."

"Okay, I'll Google it," said Raith. "I brew a good cuppa, too." He gave Mike an 'I forgive you' kiss and put the kettle on.

While he was out of the room, Phil asked Mike for more details about the so-called voluntary interview.

"A traditional interview takes too much time

and money," Mike explained. "This is still under caution, though. He'll get the 'You have the right to remain silent' stuff, and he can have a lawyer present. The duty solicitor's okay—I checked to see who was on—but I'm sure they'll let me stay with him all the time, with him havin' a clinical diagnosis, and they won't want to seem as though they're makin' life tough for a guy who's queer either."

"Being gay comes in handy sometimes?"

"Surprisin'ly, yes."

"Will Flaxby be there?"

"No," said Mike.

He'd had a fraught conversation with his ex-superintendent the previous afternoon, despite Flaxby apologising for having been so secretive.

"Well, what the fuck, Clive? You could have told me and kept me in the loop."

"Just like you did two years ago? You've a short memory, Mike."

There was silence. Mike didn't have a response; he'd kept important information to himself.

"Look, Mike. I couldn't tell you. You're his lover, for goodness sake! And apart from that, if Fraud Squad bigwigs think that I'm feeding you information, they'll make sure that I don't have any to give."

"Aye," Mike admitted, common sense replacing irritation. "I know. Look, will you be around tomorrow when we come in for the VI?"

"No."

There was something in the super's voice.

"Will Fortune be there?"

"In the building, yes."

"Shite!"

Detective Chief Inspector Fortune had been Mike's immediate superior in CID, and was the last of the station's homophobic cops. If the species was going to die out, Fortune would ensure its extinction was as painful as possible. For others.

"Then why couldn't they have let the VI take place here?" Mike asked. "Doesn't have to be the station."

"In a nutshell, they felt it would be too cosy to have it at your place. They don't want to be accused of bias. They want to keep it formal."

"Oh, and does keepin' it formal apply to fuckin' Fortune, too?"

"I'll have a strong word, Mike. I'll make sure he's perfectly polite to both of you."

"Clive?"

"Mm?"

"He didn't do it. I know he didn't."

"You sound like someone whose son has just been caught red-handed. 'He didn't do it', and he stands there holding the knife."

"Brush, not knife. And I know he didn't do it."

"That's what they all say, Mike."

Flaxby ended the call.

* * *

The interview started badly but got better.

Mike didn't recognise the duty sergeant. *Things are changin'*, he thought to himself, and followed that thought with another: *Not quickly enough!*

Detective Chief Inspector Fortune came striding into the reception area.

"Well, Mr Angells," he said, placing far more emphasis than necessary on Mike's title—the last time they'd met, Mike had been an inspector. "And your… friend."

Mike acknowledged the DCI with a curt nod,

then told Raith, "Come on, luv. They need to search you."

"I'm not a fucking drug mule," said Raith.

"Not that kind of search, but we can accommodate your needs if you'd like us to, sir," said Fortune, with exaggerated politeness.

Raith bristled beside Mike, who'd had more practice dealing with Fortune's innuendos. Dismissing this one, he gently pushed Raith towards a detective he recognised from the previous day.

Three hours later, they were on their way home. There was no charge, but once again, Raith was told to make himself available for questioning. And no, he couldn't have any of his hardware back just yet. The investigation was continuing.

It was early evening and growing dark as Mike swung his Fiesta round the final bend of Tun Beck Lane. A very different sight met him than the one that, only yesterday, had met Phil. It was just as surprising, though. The BOTWACers had been busy.

Festoons of red, green and yellow lanterns decorated houses and were strung across the narrow street. A brazier borrowed from the Raku potter glowed in front of Raith's studio. It lit up silver letters spelling *Happy Anniversary*. The letters glinted on the studio door.

The sight took Raith's breath away.

"It's not our anniversary 'til tomorrow, Phil," he managed to say as Phil walked over and guided him to a chair.

"Well, we'll celebrate it early, heh?" said Phil.

The smell of chilli, cooking in a huge pan on another brazier, filled the air. And—bought from the Tunhope Arms, the inn where, one year previously, Raith and Phil had exchanged vows—

several crates of beer and lemonade were waiting to be drunk.

"Well done, you," Mike said quietly to Ross.

"I had to do something," Ross replied. "Phil was thrilled. We've been at it all afternoon. Everyone loves Raith. They all mucked in."

Guitars and fiddles appeared, and the party got under way.

At midnight, someone yelled, "Last waltz!"

"Go on!" said Mike, pushing Phil up. "Take him for a turn on the dance floor before he turns into a pumpkin."

A couple of people wondered who would lead. Mike and Ross had no such doubts.

* * *

"I was going to take you away tomorrow. Today," said Phil, when he and Raith lay in bed together. "The tickets are in my jacket."

"Oh!" said Raith tearfully.

"I love you, Raith. And so do Ross and Mike. You know that."

"Yes."

"And all the people here. They love you, too."

"In a different way."

"In a different way."

"I like the way you love me best."

Phil's lips touched his, and he opened his mouth to be kissed. He altered his position. Phil scrabbled in a drawer in the bedside table and gently but steadily inserted a strawberry scented finger. Then two. An action he made regularly at work, but it never felt like this. Here, in this flower-patterned bedroom, he was met with miniscule resistance. He gently withdrew both fingers then, a little more forcefully, inserted them again. When he was completely sure that Raith was ready, he hooked Raith's legs over his shoulders and made love to the sound of satisfied moans.

"It's already our wedding anniversary, isn't it?" said Raith later, eyes still closed.

"Yes."

"Well, that was a nice present."

He hadn't even asked where Phil had intended to take him.

* * *

In the bedroom across the landing, the focus was on words, not actions.

"They let him go, though, Mike. They've not found anything to charge him with."

"Not yet. But he's got the means. He's got the opportunity. I mean, he could be buildin' a bloody rocket in that mess of a studio, and we wouldn't be any the wiser 'til the thing bust through the roof. As far as they're concerned, it could be full of fake stuff."

"But he hasn't any motive."

"That's not how it works, Ross. First you eliminate all the people who don't have means or opportunity. Then you start lookin' for motive."

There was silence for a while.

"Look, I know he didn't do it. I was watchin' his face when you showed us that picture on the internet. Not a flicker. Sumthin' would've shown. What you see with Raith is what you get. It's one of the things I love about him, even if it makes him bloody annoyin' at times."

"You don't think he's out of the woods then?"

"No, I don't."

"But surely when they go through his phone records and his computer log, they'll see he hasn't done anything wrong."

"Takin' his stuff's only the start. Fraud investigations can go on for months. Years. Seein' who he's met. Talked to. And you've sumtimes said it yourself: transactions in the art world are often secretive, linked to tax evasion, money launderin', organised crime... The players are into big money."

"So what are you saying? That they'll keep digging 'til they find a motive?"

"Maybe."

"Maybe?"

"What do you mean? I know that 'maybe' tone of yours."

"Well, why are they focusin' on Raith? You're his agent. His best friend, too. How come they're not showin' any interest in you?"

* * *

'They' were.

Later that Thursday morning, they shared their interest. The officer delegated with the task of investigating Ross seemed to have been taking lessons from Detective Chief Inspector Fortune. He wasn't up to the master's level yet, but given time... Ironically, he offered his information in what had been Mike's office. Four men from the Fraud Squad were squashed inside it.

"Ross Whitburn-Howe," he said. "Thirty-six. Born Chester. Stockbroker father. Mother a retired solicitor. Gains a First in History of Art at Manchester. Spends the next three years at a gallery in Amsterdam. Specialism: seventeenth-century Dutch flower painters, for God's sake. Real macho stuff. Returns to UK—Assistant Curator at Durham Gallery of Antiquity and Fine Art. Meets Balan, who has just completed a Fine Arts degree in Newcastle. Sees Balan's potential…" He paused for innuendo to take effect. "…and gets Balan work as a sculptor's assistant. Starts promoting Balan's work. Meets Angells on a case. Items missing from the gallery. Angells is the investigating officer. Within a year, they're married and living in Tunhead."

"Civil partners, Bryn," someone interrupted.

"Civil partners, then. Same difference. Whitburn's pretty business savvy. Buys up the other village houses for a pittance. Rents them to his many contacts, one of these being Balan. Starts his own gallery in Gateshead. Buys, sells…"

"Okay," said a man who'd been listening behind closed eyelids. "Can we have more on the relationship with Balan. Personal and professional."

"Sure, sir. Basically, Balan's a nutcase, a walking disaster. Whitburn does his PR, acts as his agent, does everything except tuck him into bed at night. Actually, he does that, too. When they use hotels, they share the room. According to Flaxby, they don't play humpty dumpty between the sheets with each other, though."

"Flaxby said that?" asked the detective with the closed eyes.

"Well, not in so many words."

"No." There was a hint of criticism in his tone. Of his junior colleague, not of Flaxby, and not of Ross and Raith. The hint wasn't taken, though.

"The relationship is apparently platonic, though God knows how it can be: all four of them are gay. It seems that Whitburn fucks with Angells. Balan fucks with Angells and with Roberts. You could say that they've equal shares in the gardening duties, but not in the bedroom ones."

"Okay. We don't need the housekeeping details. Let's get back to the finances. Presumably, Whitburn takes a hefty cut when Balan's work is sold. You say he's business savvy. What's the state of his finances? Does he need a cash injection?"

"No. I don't see money as a motive, despite some recent problems."

"Problems?"

"Balan's work is the money spinner at the gallery. Exclude it from the takings and the gallery turns a small profit, but no more than that. Also, they've spent over a hundred grand in the last couple of years making the house next door and the Whitburn-Angells property into one place large enough for the four of them. Also, of course, Angells resigned from the Force. He works a few hours a week as an IAM examiner, but that won't even pay for condoms. Two years out, so he's over ninety thousand down. So there's been a lot of outlay, but there's also a hell of a lot of income, and they pool their financial resources. The biggest contributor is obviously Balan. Roberts is a consultant doctor. Surgeon. Highly thought of. High income."

"NHS or Private?"

"Mainly NHS. Clearly doesn't see the need to supplement his contribution to the kitty with many private patients, although he does have some. And, of course, none of the four have dependents."

"What about the lets from the houses?"

"Low rents. They obviously don't feel they need to set high ones."

"So, you're saying what? That they don't

need money, but that, if they *should* want some, Whitburn would be the brains behind obtaining it by fraud, assuming Balan's involvement?"

"Well Whitburn's not the brawn, that's for sure."

The senior officer looked briefly at his colleague, then closed his eyes again.

"Should we bring him in, sir?"

"No. He's certainly interesting, but just keep the focus on motive for now. Keep digging. What's Balan's motive? Whitburn's motive?"

"Well, one thing's certain," added Bryn. "If those two are dabbling in the money laundering business, Whitburn won't be tucking Balan up with bedsheets. He'll need a shroud."

The man in charge opened his eyes, stretched and said, "Let's move."

His colleagues prepared to leave.

"Bryn," he said. "One moment…"

* * *

The fact that he'd been reprimanded, albeit quietly and out of the hearing of others, annoyed Bryn Baker. *So the DS thought I was homophobic, did he? Why should he care!* he thought, for the twentieth time.

Resentment resulted in action. He spent the rest of the day searching for Raith's motive. By the evening debriefing, he felt he'd found it.

"Some of this is fact," he began, "and some is supposition. This part's fact.

"Balan's parents came to England in 1978 from Barranquilla in Colombia. The question is, why? Now, as well as FARC, which everyone has heard of, there was a Colombian guerrilla movement called M-19. It was founded in seventy-three. Ideologically, it was a mix of Marxists, social democrats and radical liberalists—a sort of melting pot for people who were anti right-wing for one reason or another. Eventually, in 1984, they saw the error of their ways and signed a ceasefire with the government. At that point, they could legally compete in politics. Balan's father was an intellectual, a left-wing liberalist. In the seventies, he was a member of M-19."

"Holy shit!" said one of the others.

"Now, it seems that Balan senior—Balaño to give him his proper surname—didn't like the way M-19 got its manifesto across. That is, he didn't approve of the kidnappings, ransoms and sabotage that went on. So, somehow—and I can't discover how—he gets passage to England with his wife and two kids. Balan and a brother are born later, here. All legit from this end. But I'm speculating that strings were pulled and that there might be people who don't like him."

Baker took two photographs out of a folder and passed them round.

"Raith Balan is around the same age his father was at the time all this is happening. Raith is darker skinned, but the resemblance is striking. Raith's pretty well known. I'm wondering if someone saw his picture, got curious and followed the curiosity up."

"Why? Who?"

"Well, how does this sound? The Colombian cartels and the Eastern European ones aren't the best of friends. Mr Colombian knows that Mr Russian wants to sink his profits into Russian artwork. He gets Balan to fake the artwork. He sells, privately. Mr Russian buys, privately. Mr Colombia's laughing. He, or his cartel, gets the money *and* scores one over the Russians."

"It's spec."

"Yes, but it wouldn't be the first time. It would explain why no payment for work done is finding its way into the Tunhead bank account. Balan doesn't get paid. He paints to keeps his father safe from some Colombians who've recognised he's Balaño's son. 'Do this, or we'll tell our friends back home where your mum and dad are living'."

"Blackmail. It's possible."

"It is, yes."

The SIO was a detective sergeant called Nick Seabrooke. He considered the idea.

"If that *is* what's happening, Bryn," he said, "and I'm not one hundred per cent saying we should run with it, it's not just Balan Senior who's in danger. If the Eastern European cartels are involved and they discover Balan Junior's part in the deception, there'll be more blood than paint on his studio walls. He needs a good talking to. I'll drive over there tomorrow. Well done, though. Let's leave it for now."

The sergeant phoned through to Tunhead and arranged to visit the foursome the following afternoon.

Chapter 4

DS Seabrooke drove unhurriedly along the winding Tun Beck Lane. It struck him that, if people did want to hide their nefarious carryings on, this would be the ideal place to do it. Miles off the main road and nothing but sheep as witnesses.

Mike answered the door, showed his visitor into the kitchen and offered to make a pot of tea. The offer was due to politeness, but it was something else as well. As Seabrooke knew, Mike was offering him an opportunity to get a feel for the four men and how they lived. It brought home to him that he was dealing with at least one man who knew how policing worked, even if art fraud hadn't been the ex-inspector's line.

Whatever Seabrooke had been expecting, though, this wasn't it. He wasn't homophobic, but he wasn't gay either, and he'd somehow thought that a house occupied by four gay men would be... well... different.

The first thing that caught his eye was the duty rota pinned on the wall opposite his chair: cleaning the loos, mopping the kitchen, hoovering, dusting... The second was that every time Raith's name was on the list, it was written in upper case letters, highlighted in pale blue and emphasised with exclamation marks. He fought an inclination to smile. He caught Mike watching him—his amusement at this touch of domesticity had been spotted.

Slowly, the troops filed in. Raith's hostility was palpable. Ross was nervous, but whether that was from guilt or 'normal' interview anxiety, Seabrooke was unsure. Ross's handshake was firm, though, cool on the palm and strong. Phil's was, too, and Seabrooke was aware of Phil's appraising look. There was nothing sexual in it. He was sure of that.

Mike passed tea around—mass-produced mugs this time, not the ones with sassy handles made by Raith—and sat a little way off. The others sat round the kitchen table.

And so, a good hour later, he got to the photographs he'd brought.

"I know," he said slowly to Raith, "that when ex-inspector Angells left the Force, your ex-lover and an ex-con got together and nearly killed him. I know they beat him up badly, and I imagine that not a day goes by when he doesn't think about it."

Raith glanced at Mike and nodded.

"If you've faked paintings bought by the people I've been telling you about, you won't be around to think about what they have done to you."

He placed three photographs on the table in front of Raith.

Raith sucked in his breath. "It wasn't me," he whispered, eyes still on the photographs. "Phil?"

"Take him out, Phil." Mike spoke for the first time since he'd offered to make the drinks and had introduced the others. "Go on. Get him out of here." He sounded angry.

Phil did as Mike said. Mike waited until Phil and Raith were well out of earshot.

"Are you tryin' to sign his fuckin' death warrant?" he said savagely. "He didn't do it. But if that's the stupid line your team is takin' and these damn cartels hear of it—which they will, cos that's the way the grapevine works—they'll think the same as you! You're right. If they think he's conned them, they'll kill him. Slowly. Painfully. It'll make what happened to me look like child's play. There's not a safe house in the country that'd keep him out of their hands. Jesus Christ!" Mike pounded the worktop in fury. "Jesus! You stupid fuckin' idiot! Shite!" He went to the window and stared out.

"Have you finished?" asked the sergeant calmly.

Mike didn't answer. Seabrooke repeated his question.

"Yes," Mike said dully.

"I don't think he did it either. It was obvious he didn't know about his father's involvement in M-19, and without that knowledge, there's no blackmail motive."

Mike faced him. "Why did you go on at him then? Why did you scare him like that?"

"Because of you," Seabrooke said, turning to Ross.

"Me?" asked Ross, astonished.

"Because, from what I understand, you pull all Balan's work strings. You could have suggested it… he'd have gone along with it. You seem to be in charge of all the finances round here. You manage four incomes, a gallery, these Tunhead lets… I imagine you'd know of ways to hide large sums of money."

Ross was speechless.

"I'm a businessman," he finally said. "Yes, I might know how to make a few sharp deals to avoid the taxman—avoid, not evade—and, yes, I probably could make a few fast deals in the art world, but this is streets away from what I'd do. Raith's… special. He's one of the greatest guys I know, and I've known him a long time. I would never jeopardise his happiness, let alone his life! We've got a wonderful thing going on here." He pulled his sleeve up and pointed to the tattoo on his upper arm. Raith had had a similar one on his neck: a blue lemniscate entwined around a red heart. "Mike's got one too," Ross said. "And Phil. It's an infinity heart. It symbolises the way we live our lives—with honesty, openness, passion—and, most of all, with love, and you know what they say about love. I don't need the money. *We* don't need the money. I do need Mike and Phil and Raith. I'd never hurt Raith… I might hurt anyone who hurt Raith," he added after a moment's pause.

"Well, you might try!" Mike ruffled Ross's hair affectionately.

Ross smiled at Mike. Clearly, he wasn't top of the kitchen lists for jobs depending on brute strength.

The simple gesture and its response convinced Seabrooke. He'd already been pretty certain, anyway.

"In that case," he said, smiling too, "it might be better if we work together and find out who did do this as quickly as possible."

"What?" said Mike. Yes, he'd heard correctly. He grinned. "More tea? Nick, you said your first name was?"

This time, he used Raith's handmade crockery.

* * *

Nick Seabrooke drove back to the fraud squad's temporary office in Warbridge, personal rather than professional issues on his mind. What *did* 'they' say about love? Mostly, that it was the same as sex.

Well, he knew it wasn't. He knew people, or rather, he knew *of* people, who wanted romance but not sex. Folk who were happy with hugging and kissing, perhaps, but not with penetration. That didn't, he felt, describe him, though. He'd never had a desperate urge to kiss another person, and he'd never felt sexually aroused at the sight of anybody either. He was, he'd decided, one of the growing band of perfectly normal people who identified as ace—*a*sexual—and, probably, as *a*romantic, too. He was totally happy with the labels. So from a certain point of view, what 'they' and Ross said about love was irrelevant.

And yet, that little uncomplicated gesture—Mike ruffling Ross's hair—and Ross's affectionate look in response... He'd witnessed something unmistakeable and, he realised with a slightly disturbing pang, it was something he didn't have. It was more than just close friendship.

There was no duty rota hanging in his kitchen, no name highlighted in blue. There was no sitting cosily round the kitchen table to discuss the day's events. There was no... he pictured Cromarty's interior. Not what he'd expected. But, then, what had he expected? Fluffy pinkness everywhere? Dark, manly colours to make a macho point? No, but not that curious mixture of functional and frolicsome either. A pristine kitchen, ergonomically designed. Spotless, modern appliances, a beautifully laid stone floor, bowls of fruit, half-tiled walls in delicate colours... and a calendar picture that would be perfectly at home on the cover of a porn mag, a tea towel hanging on the rack with, presumably, the same nude model showing off his wares, mugs on the draining board with handles that would make you grin or grimace, and through the kitchen's patio doors, a well-tended garden that... He gave the garden some thought. A little stream, Tun Beck probably, ran through it. Few flowers, no trees, but who needed trees when you could look out onto... what? How would he describe the 'what'? There were several things that resembled small trees, crafted with iron, occasionally with wood, and the 'trees' bore 'fruit'. But amongst the shells and pompoms and ribbons and dangling pottery objects that made no sense, there was at least one pottery penis and several scrotums crafted from clay. Nick had averted his eyes and seen Mike watching him. As he parked his car, he wondered what Mike had thought. More pointedly, he wondered what *he* had thought.

Ross's choice of words echoed in his mind: *honesty, openness, passion—and, most of all, love.* He didn't miss sex, but did he miss love?

* * *

That evening, the four men sat round the kitchen table again. A few bottles of party beer remained. Ross opened them.

"So can I have my things back?" asked Raith, taking a pale ale.

"No, luv. Officially, you're still a suspect. *The* suspect. And you'll stay the suspect 'til they rule you out."

Raith's face fell.

"But experienced cops run with feelin's as well as evidence, and the sergeant's are sayin' that you didn't do it," Mike assured him.

"So it's okay?"

"No, but it's more okay than it was yesterday."

Raith ran with that encouraging glimmer. "In that case, I'll get a bit of your present," he said to Phil. "We can eat it while we talk." He left the room.

"Eat it while we talk?" echoed Phil, puzzled.

"You'll see," said Ross.

"You know what it is then?"

"Yes. We had to test it. Like official tasters at court. To see if we survived."

"Why? What's in it? Arsenic?"

"Possibly. He had a little difficulty reading the ingredients."

"It is edible, isn't it?"

"Theoretically."

"We're relyin' on your medical knowledge, here, Phil. If we start screamin' with stomach pains in the middle of the night, that is."

"You know digestion's not my line. Oh!"

Raith came in, bearing a tray, which he placed on the table. "I felt too down to give it to you yesterday," he said. "I didn't feel like eating it."

'It' was a heart-shaped cake, covered in white icing and decorated with little hearts.

"I made it," said Raith. "I made the hearts, too."

Phil took out his phone, stood up and took a photo. "It looks fantastic, Raith. That's a wonderful present!" He gave Raith a squeeze and a little kiss.

"Almost too good to eat!" said Mike, with meaning.

"Oh no, we'll have to eat it now," said Raith innocently. "I don't know how long it'll keep."

"Pass me a knife," said Phil. He squared the heart off and cut the square into quarters then eighths. "Here you are, Mike," he said. "Have a

39

piece. No, have two!" He piled a second portion on Mike's plate, with meaning.

They chatted between bites and fought over who would have the trimmings. Then it was back to business.

"Am I in danger?" Raith asked. "Tell me. Honestly. These cartels..."

"No," said Mike, with more certainty than he felt. "Why should you be in danger?"

"Because these cartels might think the same as the police did, and think I was involved. They might be looking for a tetra-thing. They might hit on the Colombian connection too."

"That's three 'mights', Raith. It doesn't pay to think in terms of 'mights'. You'll just make yourself sick with worry."

"In other words, I am in danger. I'm not entirely stupid. If a four-man police crew can make me their prime suspect, then a fucking gang of dealers and whatever else they are can do it too. I don't want to end up like those people in the photographs. They didn't even look like people. I just want to live here with you three. I want to feel safe."

"Look, Raith—"

"No. I'm scared. I can put it behind me for bits of the day, but I'm scared."

"Raith, listen," said Mike, crouching down and taking both Raith's hands into his own. "We'll find out who did these fakes. We will!"

Raith didn't look convinced.

"Nick is goin' to pass on everythin' he knows to us. Unofficially, but he'll do it to speed things along. He knows that for him and his crew, this is one of many cases. They've probably got a dozen different investigations goin' on. We've just got this one. We can work on it twenty-four-seven. Ross can make enquiries. You know he's got contacts and he understands this stuff. Phil and I can follow up his leads."

"So it's a case of getting to them before they get to me?"

"We'll get there first."

"Promise?"

"Promise. Absolutely. Totally."

There was a pause. Raith ran a fingertip round the plate but didn't eat the crumbs. He sighed.

"I want to go to bed, Phil."

"Come on then, love."

They hugged Ross and Mike and went upstairs to their flower-patterned bedroom.

"You made him a pretty big promise, Mike," said Ross. "Are you sure we can keep it?"

"He won't know much about it if we can't," said Mike. "He'll be dead."

Chapter 5

Phil woke early, with a start. Outside, Mike's bike engine changed pitch. He was riding off somewhere. What day was it?

Of course. He said he'd have a morning call out. Mike's hours were irregular. He was an observer and examiner for the IAM, the Institute of Advanced Motorists. Nothing to do with issuing driving licences. The courses and sessions honed the skills people already had. Mike worked with car drivers and, more to his liking, other bikers.

Well, he obviously survived your cooking, Phil thought, looking fondly at the sleeping man beside him. He got up quietly, used the bathroom, dressed and went downstairs. Ross was already up, in the kitchen.

"Heard you get up," he said, passing Phil a cup of tea.

"Cheers. You're not poisoned either, then," Phil jested.

"No. It was surprisingly tasty, wasn't it? I'd get him to bake cakes more often, but it was a bit of a nightmare."

"Oh?"

"You nearly ate Plaster of Paris instead of flour."

"Grief! I'd rather have his chilli and rice. At least we know what's in it. I'm surprised he didn't sprinkle chilli pepper on the cake."

"I hid it! No. I didn't really."

"Well," said Phil, becoming serious, "what are we doing today? I heard Mike ride off…"

"He'll be back around midday. We can get on with things here. You and I can, anyway. Raith won't be much use."

"Well, he's not going to feel like working in the studio, Ross."

"No. Give me five minutes. I've an idea."

He quietly let himself out.

The idea worked. Ten minutes later, Ross shook Raith awake and asked him if he'd mind getting up and giving one of the BOTWACers some help with redecorating. "Just 'til midday. She could do with an extra pair of hands."

"Are you sure you don't want me helping here?" asked Raith.

"I think we'll be fine," said Ross earnestly.

A little later, as Raith went off to help, Phil asked, "Did he realise?"

"I'm not sure. I think he did, because I didn't get his usual groans and moans. He probably realised he'd be better out of the way."

"Mm. Do we continue what we started doing yesterday?"

"Yes, according to ex-Detective Inspector Angells."

"He must have been a bugger to work for."

"He still is a bugger."

"Naughty!"

* * *

"I need a break," said Ross, midmorning, and stretching.

"Me too. While we're having it, can you tell me

why money laundering is linked to art? I know that artworks can sell for enormous sums of money, but why the criminal involvement?"

"Well," said Ross, refilling the kettle, "it's partly tradition and partly the nature of the industry—the lack of regulations. Tea or coffee?"

"Coffee, please."

"Art transactions have always been somewhat secretive. Selling through a third person. Proxy bidding at auctions. Works disappearing into private collections for years at a time, surfacing with questions about provenance. I suppose that, in some ways, secrecy is built into the system."

The kettle switched off.

"Here." Ross handed Phil a mug.

"Cheers. And the regulations?"

"There aren't many. That's the problem. Not compared to other ways of sinking money anyway. I mean, property transactions need names and deeds. Casinos and banks are well regulated. Relatively, that is. Art? The EU made some attempt to regulate the system a few years ago. Galleries have to report anyone who pays for a work with more than seven thousand five hundred euros in cash, and we have to file suspicious transaction reports, but for many dealers and clients, secrecy is par for the course. Also, you're dealing with items that are portable. You can't roll up a two-million-pound mansion, put it in your suitcase, and hand it to someone the other side of the world. You can roll up a canvas though."

"So it doesn't happen so much with ceramics— the sort of things Raith usually does?"

"It happens, yes, but canvas is much easier to stow away."

"I see. So, drug dealers, arms dealers, traffickers…" Phil paused. The mention of traffickers stopped him from continuing.

Ross reached over and squeezed his arm encouragingly. The four men had been involved in an incident of trafficking the previous year, and Phil had suffered most.

"These… criminals," Phil continued, "they can hide their illicit profits in artwork that they can transfer… well, anywhere, and nobody's any the wiser."

"Yes. As the more traditional avenues for money laundering become more regulated, the more they use art. There's a lot less scrutiny."

"But you… I mean, you buy and sell all the time. You don't do things in secret, do you?"

"Sometimes I do, yes. As I say, it's the nature of the beast. But not the kind of transactions and sums we're talking about here, and not for the same reasons. It would be more that…" Ross searched for an example. "Say someone has an heirloom, a valuable painting and they keep it in a bank vault. They need to raise some cash but, for reasons best known to themselves, they don't want anyone to know that they're selling off their assets. You know of someone, not by name, just on the grapevine, who is looking for a painting by that very artist. Private seller. Private buyer. No names. No one is any the wiser."

"So it doesn't go down on the books?"

"That would depend. It could just be listed as 'private collection'."

"Sounds dodgy, Ross."

"I saw more of that sort of thing when I worked in Amsterdam. It was an eye opener. I might do a dodge with my business expenses at times, but that's the extent of my illegal activity these days. I mean, if Mike found out, he'd go ballistic."

Phil didn't look too convinced.

"Come on, Phil! The paintings in Gateshead sell for hundreds, or a couple of thousand at most. Not the kind of sums we're talking about. Also, they're local artists mainly. Raith's the only person with an international reputation, and that's for ceramics, not oils, acrylics and watercolours. My stock might be good for money laundering a handkerchief. A king-size duvet set? No way." He drained his mug. "Do you want another cup?"

"No thanks. Best get back to the grindstone."

* * *

Mike rode home around twelve thirty, as expected. At one, Ross phoned to see if Raith was returning to Cromarty for a bite to eat.

"When?" Ross asked down the phone. "Did you speak to them? And what happened?"

Phil could hear the concern in his voice.

"No. Thanks." He rang off. "Raith left around eleven with two men," Ross explained. "Alice answered the door. They said they were police. They showed ID. They asked for Raith. With the police having been round the other day, she didn't question it. She called Raith to the door and went back inside. She assumed the men had called here first."

"And had they?" asked Mike.

"No."

"Odd," said Mike. "Nick didn't say anything about callin' Raith back in today."

He phoned Warbridge station and asked if Raith was there. He wasn't.

"Are the London lot around?" he enquired. He

asked to be put through to them, and Seabrooke answered.

"Raith left earlier this mornin' with two men," Mike said. "Are they yours?"

Some words they couldn't hear.

"Is any other branch involved?" Mike asked. More muffled words. "Put the desk back on."

Ross and Phil exchanged glances. There was urgency in Mike's voice.

"Is Flaxby in?" Mike asked when the duty sergeant picked up. "Put me through... Come on, Clive... Clive? Raith left at eleven o'clock with two men claimin' to be police. It's nuthin' to do with the fraud squad, and there's no other branch involved."

Mike answered "Aye" and "No" a couple of times. Then he disconnected.

Phil's expression told Mike he didn't need to explain. Phil wasn't Raith. You didn't place your hands on Phil's shoulders and tell him "Don't worry. Everything will be all right."

"They're sending a car over straight away," said Mike. "I don't think those guys were cops."

"Oh, God," was all Phil said.

All three men thought of the photographs.

A car would take a good forty minutes to arrive, even with blue lights blazing.

"Come on," said Mike decisively. "I'll talk to Alice, then join you. You two ask everyone else—residents, visitors. Did they see Raith leave? Did they see the men? Did they see the car? Ross, take the houses this side. Phil, take the other. Come on, Phil," he said. "Come on, please, luv."

Phil nodded and followed Ross out of the door.

* * *

Alice had nothing helpful to say. Two men had asked for Raith. They'd shown ID, but she hadn't really registered it, and, knowing that the police had been around a day or two before, she'd simply called for Raith and gone back inside to decorate. She'd heard Raith say "Again! Why?" but hadn't heard the answer. He'd come back in, apologised for having to leave halfway through wallpapering, and that was it. He'd left.

The men were just... men. They'd been smartly dressed. Only one of them had spoken, and he hadn't said much to her, but his accent wasn't local. It sounded southern. She hadn't noticed the car.

In fact, nobody in Tunhead had noticed anything unusual, except for one little seven-year-old boy. The lad had been visiting BOTWAC with his mam and nan. The ladies had wanted to watch the blacksmith at work, but he'd found it hot and noisy, and he'd been allowed to wait outside.

Mike was anxious, but he didn't want to intimidate the boy. He crouched so that their eyes were at similar levels. He forced himself to adopt the easy-going tone that came naturally when he chatted with his two young nephews.

"Hi," he said. "I'm Mike. You're...?"

"Robert."

"Hi, Robert."

"Hi."

High five.

"Can you tell me what you saw, too?" Robert had already told a bit of it to Ross.

"I saw the man with the long hair."

"His name's Raith."

"Raith? That's a funny name."

"It's the name of a football team. A Scottish one, Raith Rovers."

"I'm a Sunderland fan."

"Black Cats, heh? Cool!" The pleasure was genuine—Mike's dad had been a Black Cats supporter. "So…?"

"He walked to the car with the men. Then they stopped a bit. Then they got in."

"Were they walkin' slowly? Fast? Can you remember?"

"Fast."

"Was Raith in front of them? Behind them?"

"He was in front 'til they got to the car."

Mike didn't want Robert to feel that he was being interrogated. He paused and smiled.

"These men, what did they look like? Were they tall? Short? Fat? Thin?" He tried to make it sound like a game.

"Not as tall as your… er… Raith."

No, they wouldn't be. At six foot three, Raith was a good bit taller than average.

"What about—" He was going to say 'ethnicity', but changed his question to: "And were they more like Cavan or Belmont?" Two Sunderland players, one black, one white.

"Like Belmont."

White, then.

"Were they talkin'?"

"The man with the long hair was. Raith. He was, like, shoutin'."

"Could you hear what he said?"

"No. Cos I was standin' here and the man was hammerin'." He meant the blacksmith, not Raith. "But I could hear he was cross."

"When they got to the car, did you see where they sat?"

"The man with the long hair and one man got in the back. The other man was the driver."

Mike didn't wish to scare the lad by asking if

Raith's entry had looked forced. He focused on the car instead.

"What sort of car was it? Did you see?"

"It was black. With dark windows."

"Hey! That's really useful. Good spot!"

Robert looked pleased. "Only, it wasn't shiny black. Not like that car." He pointed to a parked black Mondeo.

"You mean it needed washin'?"

"No. Like my stealth plane."

Mike looked to Robert's mum for help. How was he supposed to know what Robert's stealth plane looked like?

"I think he means it had a satin finish," she said.

"Gotcha!" said Mike, turning back to the boy and smiling. "Sort of dull, but not dull."

"Aye, and it had these cool lights," Robert added.

"Cool lights?"

"Aye. They looked like tongues." He stuck his tongue out and rolled it around. He was getting cocky.

"Robert!" warned his mother.

"Well, they did, Mam. I can draw them if me mam'll lend a pen."

Robert's mother produced a pen and a diary from her bag and tore off a sheet from the 'Notes' pages. Robert drew what he thought were the car's rear lights.

"That's great, Robert. Thank you," said Mike. He didn't recognise the design, but nevertheless, it was distinctive. "You'll probably have to go through all this again when the police arrive. They're on their way."

"Aren't you the police, then?"

"No. I'm—" He wanted to say *"I'm Raith's lover,"*

but of course, he didn't. "I'm Raith's good friend."
He stood up. "I'll take a photo of your drawin', and
you give the police the original. Okay?"

"Aye," said the boy, pocketing the sketch.
"Mister?"

"Aye?"

"What colour are your eyes?"

"Me eyes?"

"Are they green?"

Mike's eyes. Even Raith, tetrachromat that he
was, had trouble painting the colours of Mike's
eyes.

"I'm not sure," he answered. "Sumtimes green.
Sumtimes grey. Sumtimes some of both." He
suddenly had a picture of Raith's eyes. Brown,
almond shaped, fringed by thick dark lashes,
worried… *"Raith, where are you?"* he almost cried
out loud, but he didn't do that, either. "What colour
do you think they are?" he asked Robert.

"Green," said the boy, tentatively. "Grey… grey
and green."

"One of each?"

"No!" the boy laughed.

"Thanks, Robert. You've been really helpful,"
Mike said, smiling. He turned to Robert's mother.
"I apologise if you thought I was police. I've
contacted the police, but we're off the beaten
track here and a squad car takes some time to
arrive. People are comin' and goin' and, also,
people forget what they saw. I doubt if Robert'll
forget though. He's a really good witness."

"Is your friend in trouble, then?" asked Robert,
pleased at being complimented.

"No," said Mike, "but if your friend got into a car
with two men you didn't know, you'd be worried
about him, wouldn't you?"

"Yeah. I'd tell Mam."

"There you are, then," said Mike, and winked. "That was the green one," he said with a grin, and went back to Cromarty.

* * *

The men had been through bad times. Times when tensions had nearly split their quad apart. Times when Mike had been so badly injured that they hadn't known if he'd still be alive the next morning. But they'd never experienced anything like this.

Phil stared out the window, too numb to even picture the wreck of his plans. He should have been sitting by the Angel Falls with Raith, watching water spill down the rock face.

Ross stood up, sat down, walked across the room, sat down again, and finally put on his jacket and went outside to ask useless, inane business questions of anyone who hadn't packed up for the night. Mike, who usually switched to autopilot when investigative skills were needed and told the others what to do, found he couldn't think of anything useful except scrolling through online driving magazines to try to identify a car with Robert's 'tongues'.

Finally, Phil spoke. "You know, I never thought I'd fall in love with him the way I did. I mean, originally, it was you, wasn't it? I liked you when we met all those years ago in Gateshead. I often thought about you. Then meeting you again in Warbridge, and you spending the nights at my place when the journey back here was too icy... I thought you were great. I still do."

"I know. Reciprocated, Phil."

"And I didn't really like him at first. I thought he

was good looking, but I thought he was the most conceited, narcissistic, 'me, me, me' person I'd ever met. And he called everybody 'Babe'! I was 'Babe'. Ross was 'Babe'. The butcher, the baker and the candlestick-maker were 'Babe'. Everyone except you was 'Babe'. You were—are—'Angel-flipping-Baby'."

Mike grinned. Raith, who had more than a slight difficulty reading and spelling, insisted Mike's surname was 'Angels' not 'Angells'. Hence the 'Angel Baby'.

"Actually, he doesn't do it so much, now," Phil added.

"Just as well. I can imagine the exchange of vows at your weddin' ceremony: 'I, Raith Rodrigo Balan, take you, Babe, to be my lawful wedded husband.' Sweet."

"Sweet, my foot! One time, I decided I'd had enough of it. I told him very firmly that I had a name and it wasn't 'Babe'. And do you know what he said?"

Mike shook his head.

"He said 'Okay, Babe'! I think that's when I realised it was hopeless. *He* was hopeless, and I might as well let him float around whatever galaxy he'd wandered into and only attempt a conversation if and when he accidentally found his way back to this one."

"Aye. I know what you mean. It was all so obvious to Ross and me, though."

"What was obvious?"

"That you had the hots for him. Sumtimes we felt like givin' you a good talkin' to, but we figured you'd work it out for yourself in the end."

"Really? How do you mean?"

"Well we knew Raith liked you. He said so. You didn't come over very often back then, but when you did, you were... all the things you are, the things Raith likes about you—sumtimes funny but, mainly, serious, thoughtful, considerate, careful— and sassy. Very sassy."

Mike smiled. Phil did too.

"He'd ask us questions about what your job entailed and he was very impressed with what you did. We could see you thought that he was a total nutter, though... and I suppose your reaction was so very out of character. That was the thing. I mean, I've seen you at work when I was at the hospital on police business and we were on the same case, on it from different angles. You deal with everybody and everythin' in the same patient, calm, carin' way, doesn't matter who or what they are, but Raith really got beneath your skin. I can remember Ross sayin' that you'd either murder him or marry him."

"I married him. One year and two days ago. Shit. Bloody hell."

Mike went and sat by Phil and placed a broad arm round his shoulder.

"I know exactly when the penny dropped," Phil said. "One time... I was here waiting for you and Ross to return from somewhere or other, and he barged in, and I sat there, looking daggers at him, and—out of the blue—he said, 'You don't like me much, do you?' And I said, 'No, not much.' Then he asked me why. So I told him. Told him he was loud, inconsiderate, selfish and that he moaned too much, and he said, totally seriously, 'But there are so many things to moan about.' It made me laugh, but he wasn't being funny. He said, 'I don't know how to handle them. Ross and Mike help me. That's why I'm here all the time. I couldn't manage if they didn't help me.' Then he said he had hoped that I'd like him because I was calm and he could see that I was kind even if I wasn't kind to him. And he just stood there, twisting his hair round his fingers, big brown eyes looking at me dolefully, and you know what? All the layers he wraps round himself just started to fall away and I started to see what you two see. That he's got so many problems. A battleground. Constantly at war with himself. That he's... as confused as he's lovely. Because he is... he is beautiful, isn't he? Face... physique... he's a good-looking guy is our Raith. Next minute, we were ripping the clothes off each other and we jumped on your bed and I didn't even have to ask. He lay on his stomach, and the rest is history.

"Where is he, Mike? What are they doing to him? I want him back here safe and sound. I want him in my arms. I want him safe in my arms. Just safe. That's all."

Mike held Phil in *his* arms. There was nothing else he could do.

Chapter 6

Ross returned.

"Everybody's asking about Raith," he said. "I'm glad it's Sunday tomorrow. It means we won't have BOTWAC visitors."

"We won't have the press either," said Mike, loosening his hold on Phil. "Flaxby's arrangin' a road block just before the junction with the six-eight-nine. Can't see reporters sloggin' ten miles along Tun Beck Lane on foot, can you? That's just for the rest of today and tomorrow, unless you want to close BOTWAC on Monday, too, Ross."

"I'll ask around tomorrow. Probably will, yes."

A couple of days' closure wouldn't impact the BOTWACers too badly. Ross's Gateshead gallery was the main outlet for the artisans' wares, though visitors could buy directly from the studios if they, like little Robert's mother and gran, visited the little hamlet.

"You know, I only sent Raith off to Alice's house because we thought he'd be no use here. If he'd stayed…" said Ross, blaming himself for what had happened.

Something clicked. "Shit!" said Mike. The others turned to look at him. "Who knew I was on a call out this morning? Apart from you two and Raith?"

"Well, the people in the IAM office, obviously," said Ross.

"And the guys in the fraud squad. Seabrooke

anyhow. When he was here yesterday, you said you'd be unavailable if there were any developments, but that we'd be here."

"Anyone else?"

"Not that I know of," said Ross.

"Me neither," said Phil. "Why?"

"Because if I'd been here, and two guys claimin' to be cops had knocked on the door, you can bet I'd have asked them some questions. Mutual acquaintances. Sumthin' for sure. They arrived after I'd left. There was no black car around, and I didn't pass one on the lane either. A couple of tractors. A couple of cars I recognised. No black C-class Merc. That's what I think it was, a Mercedes C two hundred. Wait a tic." He showed them an online photo of a Mercedes 220. "I guess you might call those rear lights 'tongues'."

"Have you phoned that info in?" asked Phil.

"Yes, in case they haven't had time to work it out themselves. It's a popular fleet car, though. There are thousands of 'em on the roads, although the satin finish is unusual. That would narrow it down to hundreds, and it'll take days, weeks to follow each one up. Assumin' it wasn't stolen."

"But, Mike," said Ross, ignoring Phil's question and Mike's depressing answer, "you're saying they wanted you out of the way?"

"Aye, they did, which means one of two things," Mike said, scrolling through his contacts.

"Who are you phoning now?" asked Ross.

"The IAM office. They'll still be there."

Someone answered Mike's call.

After the brief exchange of pleasantries, Mike asked "And were you on yesterday as well as today?"

The answer was yes.

"I can't explain now, but this is really important.

Did anybody ask when I was next on call out? Ask by name, that is? Okay, and would you have been on the desk all afternoon? Could anyone else have taken a call? Thanks. No, it's fine. I'll explain some other time, if you wouldn't mind. Thanks."

Mike disconnected and looked at Ross and Phil. Both men realised where Mike's thoughts were leading him.

"Shit, Mike, if what you're thinking's right…"

"I'm right."

"Do you think that's why Seabrooke came here? To find out when you'd be absent from Tunhead?"

Mike considered the possibility. His instincts about people were usually sound. A natural empathy and sensitivity coupled with years of distinguishing truth from lies.

"How did it come up?" he asked. "Did he ask it directly—'Will you be here tomorrow?'—or what? Was it as blatant as that?"

"I'm not sure," said Ross.

"Phil?"

"I'm not sure either."

"Well, picture the conversation. Put the actions in. Fillin' the kettle, havin' a cup of tea. Anchor the words to some actions."

"I took a call from the gallery," said Ross. "Then you said something about my needing to go into Gateshead, with not having been there for a couple of days, and I said that it was okay. I could Skype if there was anything important. Then you said that you would have to go out for a bit because you had a session with three bikers. You said you'd be back by midday, though."

"Shortly after midday," Phil corrected. He recalled the conversation too.

"So Seabrooke wasn't elicitin' any information?"

"No. It just arose out of normal conversation, and after I took the phone call."

"So he wasn't fishin'."

"No, and he didn't ask when you'd have to leave or anything."

"He wouldn't have to," Mike admitted. "He knows how long the journey takes, and he'd probably be able to work out what time I'd have to leave. I didn't take him for a bent cop, though. Not that that means anythin'." Mike sighed. "I managed to fool everyone at Warbridge station, didn't I? And I didn't even have any practice." Mike was referring to the secrets he'd kept that had led, eventually, to his resignation from CID two years earlier. He wasn't proud of what he'd done.

"But there's no reason for him to go back to base and tell them, is there?" asked Ross. "He might have texted them or phoned, but they weren't meeting up again 'til Monday morning. We don't know what he said, and we don't know if he decided to tell the others he believes us."

"But why might someone from a fraud squad be involved with the garbage who are involved in this?" asked Phil.

"It'll be the same, whatever the branch, Phil. You have to have your people on the inside. It can be the only way, sumtimes, to get a lead. And I guess, from what Ross says about the secretive way the art world seems to function, art fraud squads need people on the inside more than most."

"But this is the other way round, isn't it? It's the police who might be doing the informing."

"So it seems. It means we can't trust anybody. We're on our own again."

"True," said Mike, "but we know a little more than we knew a couple of hours ago. The garbage, as you say, definitely weren't here when I left at eight thirty and I didn't see them on the lane to the six-eight-nine. There were a couple of tractors, a couple of cars I recognised. No satin black Merc though. So, they arrive after eight forty-five. Probably quite a bit later. They want to give me time to get out of the way. But they're here before ten o'clock. They don't knock here. That means they know that Raith has gone to Alice's. They probably wait to see what happens, but they get fidgety when he doesn't come back and they know that I'm due home around dinner time. So they knock on Alice's door at eleven, give or take ten minutes—that's when the smithy demo's takin' place and Robert's standin' outside the forge. So, puttin' that together, unless they're parked up sumwhere, they're drivin' along the six-eight-nine before nine forty-five and again after eleven fifteen."

"We don't know the direction they took, though, or if they left the trunk road for the motorway," said Ross.

"True, but when I rode home, there were traffic cops hidin' on the bridge near the bottom of Ellerby Hill. You know they like to catch people out there. I doubt that these guys were caught speedin'—I imagine they'd have a snooper—but you never know. You've been caught out there even though you know that's where Traffic like to hide! Let's assume these guys aren't local. You've never heard of anybody local bein' involved in sumthin' like this, Ross, and you've worked in the North East for years, and I never heard of anythin' like it either. I'm pretty confident they're from out of town. It's likely that they head along the six-eight-nine towards the motorway. It's *un*likely that they'll know about Ellerby Hill. Okay, they might have false plates. They might have even driven along at thirty miles an hour, but you know what I'm goin' to say…"

"If it's the only lead you've got, you follow it," said Ross.

"So let's phone Flaxby and get him to follow it."

Mike contacted his old super and passed on his thoughts about the car. Flaxby agreed to follow it up.

"There's another thing," said Mike, "but I don't want to talk about it on the phone or anywhere in public. Can I come and visit you at home, please?"

He hadn't enjoyed asking that. The last time he'd been in Flaxby's house, he'd left his blood and half a tooth on the study carpet. Raith had suggested he repair the tooth with an emerald one—to bring out the green in his eyes. The idea had received a very negative reaction.

Mike was friends again with the super, but both of them knew that the great mutual respect that had been a feature of their working relationship would never be restored. They agreed a time, and closer to it, Mike set off for Warbridge. He took his car. He wanted to divorce 'this' time from the last one. Then, he'd ridden his bike. Flaxby had slung the crash helmet after him when he'd thrown Mike out of the house.

The super's wife, Dorothy, opened the door and gave Mike an enormous hug. She'd always fought his corner. An amateur potter with a penchant for paintings, she knew Mike's men socially, not professionally. She'd always been fond of 'the Angel Band', as she liked to call them, and she recognised the strength of the ties that bound the quad together. She ushered Mike into the living room where Flaxby was waiting, offered a drink, which he declined, and tactfully withdrew.

Mike was glad he wasn't in the study. Diplomacy perhaps? He wondered if anyone had hoovered up the remains of his tooth.

"Thank you for seein' me, Clive," he said, and began to explain.

When Mike stopped speaking, Flaxby said, "You could be jumping to conclusions."

"I've jumped to bigger ones and been right."

Flaxby nodded. He'd always trusted his ex-inspector's judgement. Despite the things that had happened, he saw no need to question it now.

"Okay, Mike," he said. "I'll find out everything I can about the London crew. If I come up with anything suspicious, anything, I'll let you know. I'm not involved with their fraud investigation—you know that—but obviously, Raith's disappearance, or, rather, Raith's kidnapping, is CID, and I can put my fingers in the pie."

"Would it compromise you, or compromise the investigation? Knowin' the four of us as you do? Knowin' me?"

"What you're asking? No."

"Thank you."

"Get home, heh?"

"Aye." Mike sighed.

Dot Flaxby came into the room in response to her husband's shout that Mike was leaving. She walked Mike to the front door.

"We'll find him, Mike," she said as she gave him another big hug. "Give Ross and Phil my love."

Mike nodded and drove home.

* * *

Raith had taken the two men's explanations at

face value. It was only when they'd reached the car and he'd tried to continue across the road that he'd realised his error. He'd wanted to knock at Cromarty to say that he was needed at the station. The men told him to get straight in the Merc. The one who wasn't driving was insistent, pressing home his point with something sharp against Raith's ribs. Raith did as he was told.

Raith was unpredictable. One Raith would rant and rave and, in anger and frustration, try to fight his way out of a dangerous situation—a reaction that, here, could have provoked unwanted intimacy with the unknown sharp object. Another Raith was stoic. There'd been times in his life when he'd had to allow events to simply run their course. This was one of them. He didn't relax, but, in a sense, he did shut down. He didn't fuss. He just let himself be driven.

They turned off the six-eight-nine and joined the motorway. He registered the fact that they were travelling south, then closed his eyes and waited. Nobody spoke for a couple of hours. It began to rain heavily.

"I need to pee," Raith said suddenly.

His minder drank the contents of a bottle in the door bin and passed the empty container over.

"I need more than a fucking Evian bottle," said Raith. "I haven't peed all day."

"Services. Leicester. Five miles," said the driver. He tossed a cagoule over his shoulder. "Put that on. Use the hood." Not an unexpected kindness— he just didn't want Raith to be recognised.

Even so, he wasn't taking chances. He ignored the main car park and facilities and, instead, pulled round to a small toilet block adjacent to the petrol station. All three men got out.

"Don't try anything," Raith was warned.

The driver made sure that the toilets were empty then waited outside. The other one, called King, entered with Raith. He removed Raith's belt. "Just in case you're thinking of playing tricks," he said, and stood near the door.

Raith loosened his jeans.

"You gay or something?" he asked. "You're going to watch me, are you?"

King made a sound like 'tut' and turned around.

Raith peed.

"I need to shit," he said.

"Raise your arms and stand still," said King. He frisked Raith. "Just in case you're thinking of leaving more than your shit in the bowl."

Raith went into the cubicle, dropped his pants and grasped the end of a wax crayon that he'd shoved up his anus when King's back was turned. He'd been using it to mark the cutting lines on Alice's wallpaper. It was too small to have made any obvious bulge and it had lain hidden in his pocket.

The cubicle partitions were plasterboard, not tiled, and the crayon made good, clear lines. Raith looked at what he'd quickly drawn and written and wondered about the stub. Could he walk with it shoved back up his arse? Yes. Could he sit with it shoved back up his arse? Yes. Could he extract it if the need or opportunity arose again? Maybe. It was worth the risk. He pushed, flushed the loo, and zipping up, opened the door.

They drove off again.

Raith had always struggled with reading and with spelling. He could reproduce individual words and numerical sequences, though, if he thought of them purely as images, and inside the cubicle, he'd quickly reproduced three. He'd glanced at the car's registration plate as he'd walked behind it to the toilet, and that was one of the things that he'd written on the wall. Drawn on the wall. The second drawing was his minder's wrist, complete with an unusual tattoo. It was more detailed than a sketch. Raith had always been observant, and he had that rare talent: the ability to represent on paper, canvas, clay—a whole variety of media—precisely what he saw. This time, he'd used a toilet wall. And thirdly, he drew Phil's mobile number, and added the two words 'Phil Help'. He didn't know if anyone would see his efforts, let alone understand that they weren't mere graffiti, but he didn't know what else to do.

He sat in the car and thought of *his* tattoos, of one in particular: the red heart, and entwined around it, the blue infinity sign. He thought of Phil and of the anniversary present that he'd left for safekeeping with Ross. He hadn't simply baked a cake. This present was exquisite: a gold wristwatch with a face and a strap fashioned by the artisans at BOTWAC, made to Raith's own design. The numbers were tiny red hearts, with the quarters slightly larger. The strap was made of interlocking infinity signs.

He sighed. He thought of Mike and Ross. Did they even realise he was missing?

Raindrops fell on the windows of the car. A teardrop fell on Raith's cheek. He turned his head aside so King wouldn't see.

The traffic grew heavier as they travelled down the M25. More lorries carried foreign number plates. The driver ignored the filters for London. They crossed the Dartford Bridge and followed the signs for the A2 and Dover. As they joined the A2, panic surged through Raith. Were they taking him abroad? No. They left the trunk road and took a far less busy route to a village in Kent called Cobham. They turned into a country lane, the intermittent houses hidden by tall hedges. They slowed down. Electric gates opened in a high wall. They sped along a curving drive edged with lime trees. Horses grazed in the paddocks. Such a peaceful scene. They pulled up in front of a large, modern mansion: 'house' belittled its size.

"Out," said King.

Raith did as he was told and was led inside. He was hungry. He was thirsty. He was stiff, but he was too hyped up to be tired. His eyes took in everything around him, especially the pictures on the walls. If these were originals, the owner of this house had assets worth a fortune.

Raith was directed to a windowless room at the back of the house. It was sparsely furnished compared to the tiled and carpeted opulence he'd glimpsed as he'd been led through. A second door led to a toilet and small sink. Someone brought a glass and jug of water, and he guzzled thirstily.

A man came in and sat down in one of the room's two chairs. Raith remained standing, glass in hand. The man seemed to be observing him, scrutinising him. Raith met and held his gaze.

"Mr Balan," he said. "You don't know me, but I believe I know you. Of you, that is. Indeed, I believe I have had some of your artwork here in this house."

There was a pause. Raith felt that he wasn't expected to show pleasure at hearing the information. What did 'have had' mean?

"My ancestry is Russian," the speaker continued, speaking calmly. "I have many works by Russian artists, too. You may have seen some as you walked through?"

Hearing the question, Raith said "Yes" and waited.

"I have two works by Chagall. I have a Malevich. I have a Kandinsky. I have several works by minor Russian artists also. Gerasimov, for example. You will appreciate that acquiring these works often requires considerable effort. The politics of my ancestral country sometimes required that canvases were hidden or smuggled across the border. You could say that I have made it my life's quest to discover their whereabouts and collect them. This pursuit costs a great deal of money. Even works by minor artists are expensive, these days. There is increasing demand, you see. I am not the only collector of such paintings. Sometimes, much as I enjoy looking at my acquisitions, I sell them on."

There was another pause. Raith could see where this was leading, but he didn't know what to say.

"One of the minor artists whose work interests me is Masha Ivashova."

Raith's face betrayed his familiarity with her name.

"Ah, you have obviously heard of her."

"Yes."

"I acquired two Ivashovas a year or so ago, privately. I can't show them to you, unfortunately, as they are, regrettably, no longer in my possession. I re-sold them. I recently tried to acquire a further Ivashova. It was a painting of a waterfall. As I say, Mr Balan, I tried to acquire it. However, it seems that there is a problem with that painting. It transpires that it isn't an original Ivashova at all. It is fake! What do you think of that?" Without waiting for an answer, he continued. "Now, what concerns me is that, in good faith, I sold my other Ivashovas—the two I bought privately—to a collector who... let us say, doesn't usually acquire artwork for the same aesthetic or nostalgic reasons that I do." He let Raith dwell on this for a moment. "Quite simply, I need to know if you painted just the one, or all three."

"None of them," Raith said quietly.

"You see," the man continued as though Raith hadn't spoken, "if you merely painted the waterfall, we could come to some arrangement. Of that, I'm sure. However, if you painted the two Ivashovas that are no longer in my possession, the two that I sold, then the situation becomes much more complex. So, I ask you again. Did you paint just the one, or all three?"

"I didn't do them," Raith repeated.

"Well, we'll talk again this evening."

And with that, Raith was left alone in the room.

His 'host' hadn't spoken angrily. Indeed, he hadn't raised his voice at all. Raith had felt the threat behind the quiet manner, though. He sat down and tried not to think about what might happen later.

* * *

"I didn't fucking paint them!" Raith shouted for the umpteenth time. He put his hand to his face and wiped away the blood. Someone, neither of the men who had driven him, had twisted Raith's long hair around his wrist then slammed Raith's face into the wall.

He yanked Raith back by the hair and did it again.

"God! Ahh." Raith panted. "I've told you," he

cried desperately. "I don't need money. I don't need fame. I don't need to prove anything to anyone. I've got no reason to do it. There must be other people who can paint like that! Aw, Jesus!"—a response to a kick in the stomach that doubled him up. He'd have vomited if he hadn't been so empty. "I didn't paint your fucking paintings! God, that hurt!"

"Leave it for now," said another man who was in the room, watching. "Get him something to eat, and shut him in for the night. You appreciate," he said to Raith "that this building has immaculate security features. We have a lot of valuable artwork to protect. We know if someone tries to get in. Likewise, we know if someone tries to get out. Sleep well."

The other man brought Raith a plate of toast, then left and locked the door. Raith was frightened and he was hurt, but he hadn't eaten for twelve hours and he was hungry. He ate the toast and was left to himself for the night. He still had the stub of crayon, but he didn't see any way to make use of it.

I probably can't get the fucking thing out now, anyhow, he thought. He'd have to get Phil to extract it. When... If...

Panic hit.

He wasn't exactly fearful of tomorrow. Raith's imagination never really spent time dwelling on the future—too many demons occurred in the present. Mental overload: he'd rammed his head against the nearest wall on many occasions. It was the only thing that had seemed to help. Then Ross and Mike and Phil had entered his life. They'd engineered some calm.

Phil was the only one who could banish the chaos completely, though. By holding him. By stroking his head and his neck. By... just being Phil. But Phil wasn't there and Phil wouldn't even know where 'there' was!

Raith tried to calm the storm that began to swirl around his tired brain but, being Raith, he couldn't. A dozen thoughts piled in together.

He sat on the chair, his head in his hands, elbows resting on the table. Mercifully, finally, he slept.

Chapter 7

The sound of the door opening woke Raith from a dream-filled, uneasy sleep.

Yet another man entered the room, with a tray, coffee and a question: "Are you vegetarian?"

A puzzled answer: "No."

Ten minutes later, the man returned with a plate of Eggs Benedict with salmon, more toast and a small bowl of fruit. He left without speaking. It occurred to Raith that they were only feeding him until they thought that he'd outlived his usefulness. He was famished, though, so he ate.

The door re-opened. The breakfast items were cleared away. The man who'd bought the paintings entered the room.

"I hope you enjoyed your meal," he said.

Raith didn't answer.

"Mr Balan, have you thought further about our conversation of yesterday?"

"What do *you* think? Of course I've fucking thought about it."

"And?"

"And what?"

"And would you like to amend any of yesterday's details?"

"I've told you. I don't know anything about your paintings. I didn't paint them."

The man sighed.

"Mr Balan, you don't seem to realise that I'm trying to help you."

"Help me! Your frigging heavies try to shove my head through the wall. They yank out half my hair. You keep me locked up here all night. That's fucking helping me?! Shite!"

"You really would be well advised to tell me what you know. Believe me, my 'heavies', as you call them, are angels compared to those in the employ of the person to whom I sold the Ivashovas." Slight impatience had crept into his voice.

"I don't know anything to tell you," Raith said, far less belligerently this time. "Oh God. I don't!" Behind his eyes flashed the photographs Seabrooke had shown the quad from the police file.

Mike always said that fear had a smell. Raith was no stranger to it. Eighteen years old. Blay Fenn Jail. Cellmates who had held him down. Fucked for the first time in his life. Raith knew what fear smelt like. He knew he must stink— of sweat, of unwashed skin, and fear. His eyes began to smart.

He shook his head. "It wasn't me," he said. He wiped his arm across his cheek to clear away tears before any weakness was spotted.

The man left. Someone relocked the door.

* * *

It was Lee Rawlins' job to check the state of the toilet block at the motorway services twice a day. He cursed when he saw the state of the partition wall. He tried to wipe the damage off with the cleaning fluids kept in the little stock room, but he couldn't. He'd have to use strong solvents, but they were locked safely away in the main building. It was pouring down. He couldn't be arsed. He'd do it in the morning.

The management didn't like graffiti. Better to dispense with the cubicle altogether. He placed an 'Out of Order' sign on the cubicle door and left a message for the cleaner who'd come in later. A few hours later, he went home.

He was finishing a cup of tea with half an eye and half an ear on the evening news. He put the cup down, not sure if he'd heard correctly. He switched to another channel to hear the item again. He didn't have long to wait. He sat up and listened closely.

"... are concerned about the whereabouts of sculptor, Raith Balan. Mr Balan was last seen getting into a black Mercedes with two men who claimed to be policemen." A photo of Raith appeared on screen, soon superseded by another one. Then came the bit that Lee had wanted to hear again. "Mr Balan is married to Philip Roberts, a doctor who has pioneered a form of reconstructive surgery using nanocarbon patches..."

Philip... Phil... He'd spent a good half hour trying to erase that very name and the rest of the drawing from the toilet wall.

There was a landline number to contact if anyone had information. It wasn't the number on the wall, Lee was sure of that. That number had been a mobile.

Coincidence? Maybe. Probably. The chances of the missing man turning up at his services were small, surely. If he phoned the police, he'd probably be sending them off on a wild goose chase. Divert their meagre resources from the real thing. He'd think about it overnight. Maybe do something tomorrow. The mess on the wall would still be there. He'd sort it out tomorrow…

The morning after his discovery, and back at work, Lee Rawlins stared at the partly cleaned wall. He made a note of the name and mobile number in his contacts, then replaced the 'Out of Order' sign—just in case. Just in case of what, he wasn't sure. He felt he was being foolish, but at the same time, he felt concerned. He was overreacting; he knew it. Self-conscious, he sat far away from anyone else to make the call. He scrolled through and clicked the 'Dial' sign.

The phone rang. He hit 'Stop' before anyone could answer. He clicked again.

A tense voice asked, "Yes?"

Tentatively, he asked if he could speak to somebody called Phil.

"Speaking," said the voice. "Who is it?"

He was embarrassed now. He was about to ask what seemed a stupid question, probably for nothing.

"Are you Doctor Philip Roberts?"

"Yes. Who's speaking? Is this about Raith? Who is it?"

Lee took a deep breath and explained. Someone else was speaking, a man with a North East accent. He answered the questions as best he could.

Had he phoned the police? No.

Did the petrol station use plate recognition technology? Yes.

Clear, terse instructions followed. When they were all given, Lee disconnected and went to ensure that yesterday afternoon's security information was still available.

* * *

Mike phoned Flaxby straight away, and in turn, Flaxby alerted East Midlands constabulary. He also did what he could to trace the owner of the car. Keeping his promise to Mike, a couple of hours later, he passed the details on.

Mike was correct. The Mercedes was a fleet car. It was registered to a successful firm of civil engineers and architects with premises in London's Canary Wharf. Officers from the Met had visited to investigate but, being Sunday, no employees were there. The officers had contacted the caretaker and studied the CCTV. None of the firm's fleet cars had driven in or out of the car park the previous day. Wherever Raith was, he wasn't there.

"But it *is* their car?" Mike asked.

"Yes, but the car was reported as stolen, Mike. Last night."

"What?" Mike said with disbelief. "That's bloody convenient. What time? Before or after that news clip?"

"After."

"Great. Lee Rawlins hears the news... they hear the news..."

"I know," Flaxby agreed, "but that's the story."

"And why would anyone suddenly want to check the location of one of the fleet cars, when the offices are closed 'til Monday mornin'?" Mike was angry, not puzzled.

"My thoughts, too. According to a spokesperson from the firm, employees are allowed to make reasonable use of the vehicles."

"And kidnappin' Raith's reasonable use, is it?"

"They claim the car was stolen from a

residential street," said Flaxby, ignoring Mike's sarcasm. "Sorry Mike."

"Not your fault, but it's a fuckin' cock up none the less. Talkin' about the Merc on the news might have alerted the bastards."

"I know, but it cuts both ways, doesn't it? The reference might have jarred Joe Public's memory. It jarred Rawlins'."

"Aye. You're right. I know. Thanks, Clive." Mike rang off.

* * *

The instructions handed out in Cobham were just as direct and terse as Mike's had been when he'd spoken to Lee Rawlins.

Burn the car.

Report it as stolen.

You two—take a couple of weeks off work. Someone might have seen you with Balan. Let's take no chances.

* * *

"So is it a dead end?" asked Phil when Mike passed on the news.

"No, luv. Just give me a minute to think, heh?"

Phil nodded.

There were too many forces involved in this for Mike—Tees, Tyne and Wear, the Met, East Mids. Liaison wasn't easy at the best of times... uncertainty about who should pull rank, the need to get your own constabulary's case-solved stats as high as possible in the tables, the feeling that it's not your problem anyway when you're already understaffed and overwhelmed. And here, the whole caboodle complicated by the thought that people who should be working for the law might be working against it.

"Okay," said Mike. "This is what we do."

Ross winced when Mike asked him to re-phone all his art-world contacts.

"I know, but last time you were enquirin' about a fake and its painter. This time, you're askin' about Raith. It's different," Mike pointed out.

Ross nodded, only for Mike to change his mind. Mike had intended to tell Phil to dig up everything he could about the firm that owned the Merc— who they'd done work for, who was on the board—everything—but a look at Phil's face showed him Phil needed a break from all this.

"Ross, can you do that instead?" Mike asked. "Phil, grab your leathers."

"Why? Where are we going?" Phil wanted to know.

"To see a man about a dog. Well, a woman about a dog and a curious motto."

There were thousands of tattoo artists, most of whom would regard a tattoo of a dog as simply stuff that paid the rent. Instantly forgettable. Raith's service station drawing had been typically detailed, however: a dog and a motto. The motto interested Mike more than the dog itself. Perhaps it was unusual enough to have jogged someone's memory. He was interested in the psychology behind the tattoo though. A King Charles spaniel seemed a strange choice of image for a kidnapper.

It was Sunday. Free, easy parking in Warbridge. He chained the bike to a lamppost and he and Phil went in to Amy's Place, a tattoo parlour.

Amy opened up specially for their visit.

"It's all round about Raith," she said. "I'm sorry. Have you heard anything?"

"Not really," said Mike.

"So, how can I help?"

Mike showed the photo on his mobile. Rawlins had sent it across to him.

"We need to find the man with this tattoo," he said.

Amy looked at it.

"You're asking for a miracle," she said. "It's just... a dog." A skilled tattooist's reaction to a basic design. Amy hadn't inked the quad's infinity hearts—they'd been simple affairs and she'd left them to her less skilled assistant—but the complex designs that covered Raith's arms and upper body, and the once beautiful design on Mike's back, were down to Amy. She looked at the two men, doubtfully.

"I know, but what about the motto below it? It doesn't look like any foreign language alphabet? Someone might remember doin' that."

"Let's look again. I was looking more at the dog."

She scrutinised the design.

"Maybe. I've never seen that before."

"How would we trace it?"

"But Mike," Phil interrupted, "even if we find the artist, how do we find the man?"

"Amy knows us. You get to know your customers. Why shouldn't he be known? Might be long odds but you'd be amazed how many crimes get solved with longer odds than these. So how would we find out, Amy?"

"Well, guys, there's a big tattoo jam next weekend at York races. Tattooists from all over the UK. You could try there."

"Next week!"

"Too late, Amy," said Mike. "We need answers sooner than that."

Amy thought.

"Well, the only other thing I can suggest is this: I'll contact a few people I know who work on the skin mags and I'll get them to put a copy of that photo on their Facebook page and anywhere else where they've got a lot of followers. If next week at York's too late, it's no use waiting till the next issues come out. And I'll try to pull in some info on my own accounts too and spread the word. Can I explain why? Can I say it's something to do with Raith?"

"By all means. Chances are that the guy we're lookin' for doesn't read the stuff you folk do, and even if he does… we're pretty desperate. Thanks, Amy."

"I'll get onto it straight away."

"Thank you, Amy."

"No prob, Phil."

The two men left.

They sat on Mike's bike and followed the six-eight-nine back towards Tunhead. Instead of turning up the little lane, Mike carried on for a few miles. He pulled through a gap by a farm gate and parked the bike behind a hawthorn hedge, out of sight of passing traffic.

"We can spare half an hour," he said in answer to Phil's unspoken question.

They walked through long grass until they reached a little lake fringed by a ring of hills. They sat together at the water's edge.

Phil hadn't spoken since they'd left Amy's Place. He didn't speak now. He just sighed and stared at the water. Finally, he put an arm round Mike's shoulder.

"Thanks," he said. "You know I think it's special here. Five minutes' walk from a busy road, and yet the traffic's just a murmur in the background.

It's peaceful here. Serene." A rueful smile. "God, Mike, I don't feel serene. I feel churned up inside. We haven't heard anything…"

"No news is good news, Phil." He knew it wasn't—not with a missing person—but it was what Phil needed to hear.

Phil nodded.

They stayed five minutes longer, gazing at the dark, still water. Phil's arm became heavier as he began to relax.

"Let's go back now, heh, and see what Ross has found out," Mike suggested.

Phil nodded. Mike stood up and transferred Phil's arm to his waist. With his own arm around Phil's shoulder, they walked back to the bike.

* * *

"Clive phoned just after you left," Ross said as soon as they got in. "The fraud crew: two of them are pretty new to it—a Bryn Baker and an Ezra McKeown. They're not new to frauds, but they don't usually handle art cases. Baker's never handled an art fraud. The other two… if we're looking for a bent cop, it's more likely to be one of them. There's Seabrooke himself, and the fourth guy's called Anthony Rybak. They've both worked on several art cases. They'll have connections… They've got unblemished records, but they are the two with the background knowledge. The more likely candidates. You look disappointed." He said that to Mike.

"Sort of. I liked Seabrooke. I'd be disappointed if it was him. If one of them is bent, though, he must be pretty good at hidin' it. There's no reason why this should be the first time."

"Did you find out anything about the firm?" asked Phil.

"Yep. Plenty. Let's have a drink and I'll tell you."

Ross told them what he'd discovered, and Phil sat back admiringly. "You're great at this sort of thing, Ross."

Ross didn't point out that he'd had a little previous practice, searching for information two years back, when Mike had wanted to put a dead man's father into jail.

"It's all there on the web, Phil. It's a very successful company. They design and build. Their projects win prizes, and they have installations all over the world. They're doing very well, but the interesting guy on the board is the chief architect, a man called Danik Amelin. His grandparents were Russian. He's fond of art—that's no secret—but the extent of his dealings… well, that's anybody's guess. The thing is, there's nothing that implicates him in any underhand deals."

"I dunno," said Mike. "It's one of those coincidences that makes you start wonderin', isn't it? The Russian connection, the art connection, the fact that Raith was kidnapped in one of his firm's cars… I want to run with it, but I don't know how, especially if Seabrooke or one of his crew is bent."

Night fell.

"You come in with us, tonight, Phil, heh?"

"It's okay, Ross. Thanks, though."

"No. Come on. We haven't done a throuple since Raith decided he was dying of pneumonia. He made it through, though. He'll get through this, as well," he added encouragingly.

"Okay. Give me half an hour."

A little later, Ross lay awake, aware of the comforting kissing and caressing that was taking place beside him. Any other night, the petting would have turned into something heavier. It wouldn't have bothered him if it had done. Once, he recalled, it would have hurt and frightened him. When? Five? Six years ago when he'd thought he would lose Mike. When Mike had told him he was sleeping with Phil as well...

More than one lover... it wasn't something Ross could do. He'd long ago decided that his participation in this polyamorous relationship was different from that of the others, but he wore the infinity heart tattoo, and he took on board its symbolism—openness, honesty, love and passion—even if, in his case, the passion was reserved for just one man. Yes, Mike could be irritatingly bossy and authoritarian, and some of the comments he levelled at Raith made Ross wince, but in other, more personal ways, he was... he was everything that Ross had ever wanted.

Mike had walked into the gallery, a detective sergeant on a case, and Ross had spent the rest of the day thinking of nothing and nobody else. He'd soon realised that Mike's outer layer was matched by something wonderful inside. Tough, efficient, completely on top of a difficult job. Gentle, kind, and loyal to a fault. Ross was still unravelling Mike's complexity, and the fact that Mike could lie in the arms of three different men and love them all was simply an indication of the intricacy of the knots.

Ross wasn't physically attracted to Phil, but he cared about him deeply. Passion, no. Love, a definite yes. He respected Phil, too, for what he had accomplished in his work, and for what he done for Raith. He was the only man who, as Raith put it, "gets inside my head as well as inside my ass." Even Mike could only claim success at one of those two.

"He's asleep," whispered Mike.

"Good," Ross whispered, and with Phil tucked between them, they slept too.

* * *

Three hundred miles away, in Cobham, Sunday evening came around. Another tray of food appeared. Raith had had all day to dwell on his situation. His brain said "Eat!" but his stomach revolted at the idea. He forced himself to push a forkful of pasta between his lips. He tried to swallow, and gagged. He tried again. The same response.

"Well, they won't have to shoot me," he told himself. "They can just let me starve to death. Would that be manslaughter? Mike would know."

He knew he had to eat something. He tried to pretend that he was somewhere else—a hotel restaurant, on holiday. He couldn't do it. Raith drew and painted exactly what he saw, right down to the last blue bubble. He sculpted exactly what he saw. He thought exactly what he saw. An artist without imagination, totally immersed in the present. He thought about the present, and pushed the plate away.

Half an hour later, the plate was silently collected. Raith waited for the door to reopen, heralding another useless session of repetitive question and answer. He was surprised that, when it did, it was only to deposit yet another tray, this one bearing a pot of coffee and more toast.

"You have to eat!" he told himself again.

He poured a cup of coffee and dunked a slice

of toast in it. He found he could swallow the mushy coffee-toast without much trouble. He ate the lot, and waited. No one came. He stretched out on the floor, and sometime in the early hours, like his lovers in Tunhead, he managed to fall asleep.

Chapter 8

Raith woke to the now-familiar sound of a door unlocking, and, stiff from a night on hard boards, he stood up. When the quiet cook set a pot of tea, another bowl of fruit, and a plate of toast and poached eggs on the little table, Raith picked up the tray and hurled it at the door.

The door unlocker was onto Raith instantly. Raith was no athlete, but hauling sacks of clay around had put muscles on his arms, and he hadn't forgotten the lessons he'd learnt years before, fighting on streets in the Midlands. Both men lost their balance and crashed to the floor, still trying to knock hell out of each other.

"Taylor!"

'Taylor' broke his hold immediately. He stood up, putting in one last kick.

"I'm sorry, sir. This idiot…" He didn't finish his sentence. He pointed to the mess running down the wall.

Raith scrambled up, wiping a bloodied nose.

"Mr Balan, you're trying my patience."

"Tough fucking shit," said Raith. "You're fucking trying mine. I know what this is about. You decided you could make a nice little pile on the side selling works to shites who should be buried in fast setting concrete… gun runners, drug dealers, people dealers… and now you're scared because you think you've sold one of them a dud.

Two duds. Well, I hope they were fucking duds, and I hope they find out and stuff you so full of your own fucking food that it busts your gut. I've had enough of this fucking shite. I want to go home. I want Phil."

He'd been shaking with the adrenalin of anger. Now, he was shaking with something else. He fought for self-control, and he lost. Head in his hands, he sank to his knees, repeating, "I want Phil."

"Somebody clean this up," said Danik Amelin, more calmly than he felt.

For the first time, he felt a shade of doubt. No, his contact had been certain. It had to be Balan. There was nobody else. Of course, Balan was right—if he had arranged the sale of fakes, it would be no use pleading ignorance. Amelin had to know. Balan was being far more difficult than he had expected. He'd have to try a different tactic, but at the moment, he wasn't quite sure what it should be.

* * *

In County Durham, Flaxby rang Cromarty's landline. One of the three, at least, would be up and around to answer the early call.

In fact, Mike was riding to Warbridge to complete an IAM stint. It was Ross who answered.

"Clive, I don't know how to thank you," said Ross, when Flaxby had passed on his information. He'd been up all night obtaining it.

"I'll give you twenty-four hours," Flaxby said. "After that, I have to liaise with the others involved. The only reason I'm giving you a head start is the concerns you've raised regarding someone in the fraud crew being bent. I'd expect the Met to follow the same line of enquiry independently—they've already been to the company's office—but I can't do anything about that."

"Thank you," Ross repeated.

* * *

Mike met his three bikers and began with an apology. He usually switched his mobile to silent and answerphone, but he hoped they wouldn't mind if he took a call himself, provided it was safe to do so: he was expecting some news. The looks the bikers gave him suggested that they thought he was anticipating childbirth. Perhaps there was a wife lying in the labour ward... A tall order. Mike, like Ross, was, had been and always would be totally gay and, like Ross, was perfectly happy with being so. Their partnership had produced more siblings—four extra for Ross, two extra for Mike—but no offspring. Mike's mum—his dad was dead—and Ross's parents couldn't give a hoot.

Phil's marriage to Raith, in contrast, had been the final straw according to *his* parents. The possibility of IVF had given his grandchild-desperate mother a tiny glimmer of hope. The marriage had snuffed it out. Better to have no offspring than one who had 'chosen homosexuality', and Phil had been disowned and disinherited. It was Phil's knowledge that his parents would disapprove of his 'choice' that, more than anything, had caused him to be riddled with guilt in his teenage years. The years had passed, and no longer caring what his parents thought, no feeling of guilt remained.

When Ross's call came through, Mike answered at the first opportunity. There was a lead of some sort. He didn't fully understand, but there was no mistaking Ross's intent when Mike and his three bikers arrived back at the IAM's small car park. Ross was standing by his car, urging Mike to hurry.

Mike apologised to the riders again.

"Usually," he said, "I keep folk waitin' for their dinner while I do a big debriefin'. I'm really sorry about all this. Would you mind if, instead of talkin' now, I contacted each of you durin' the week and debriefed then?"

They didn't. Mike knew he was guilty of taking advantage of their misapprehension, but he had to do so. He walked quickly across to Ross.

"What's this—"

Ross interrupted him. "Just make your bike safe, and sign whatever has to be signed," Ross said. "I've told them you're in a hurry, and they said you can leave your bike here."

Mike did as he was told. A few minutes later, Ross drove him to the train station.

"Phil'll tell you on the train—he's buying tickets—and I'll phone you when I get back home," he said. "There's a train due in five minutes, but it's coming from Edinburgh. Chances are it's late."

It was, but even so, Phil and Mike had to jump onto the rearmost carriage. The doors shut. They were off.

They travelled first class. Phil knew that there wouldn't be two seats together on standard, not on an Edinburgh train. As long as they kept their voices down, if they were lucky, they wouldn't be overheard.

"Have you got a drink?" Mike asked once they'd settled. "I left mine on the bike."

"I'll go and get us one," Phil answered, standing up again, "and then I'll explain why we're sitting on a train to London."

Mike's old super had been busy. He'd spent half the night digging up information on the architects and civil engineers. Unlike Ross, he'd focused on the people involved with the firm's security. They, rather than the office staff or anyone on the board, were more likely to have visited Tunhead. A couple of names had caught his eye, one in particular.

"Ex-police," Flaxby had said. "Kent constabulary. Left during his probationary period, ostensibly because police work wasn't what he'd thought it would be. I checked. He left because he and Kent didn't see eye to eye. At the time, Kent didn't allow visible tattoos, and it seems that he had one done after he joined them. I don't know where it was, or what it was, but I imagine that a tattoo on the neck or wrist would be hard to conceal all the time. Reading between the lines, though, I'd say they were glad to see him go. The tattoo was a convenient excuse. There's something else. His name is Charles King."

"Charles King? The dog!" Ross had exclaimed. "It could have been a King Charles spaniel. Is that what you're saying?"

"It's possible. I don't know."

"And more than that," said Phil, as he repeated what he'd learnt of the conversation, "Kent constabulary's badge is a star with a central circle that contains a prancing horse. Raith drew a sort of star on the toilet wall with the dog in the middle. What do you think, Mike?"

"I think that Flaxby would never have passed this on unless he was pretty sure. Christ! He's puttin' his job on the line for us, Phil. How the hell do we thank him? Even if he's wrong. To help like this... He's a bloody saint."

"Ross says he's got a cover sorted so that Clive won't get into any trouble. He'll tell us when he phones."

Shortly after, he did so.

"You're a little genius," said Mike approvingly.

"Less of the little, but yes, I've done quite well!"

After dropping Mike off at the train station, Ross had driven to the other side of town to Amy's Place.

Amy looked at him doubtfully.

"I know Mike and Phil asked if you could find the guy with the tattoo," Ross said. "I just want you to pretend you did, if we need to say so. Well, sort of."

They both knew that the likelihood that someone had recognised the design, let alone remembered whose skin it was tattooed on, was miniscule. However, if it became necessary to protect the super, it would help to pretend that Amy putting out feelers had resulted in a lead. That way, Flaxby's involvement wouldn't need to be known. Ross didn't divulge the lead's name, of course.

"Yeah, okay, Ross. On one condition."

"Yes?"

"You let me do you another tattoo when you get Raith back!"

"Heck! I suppose he's worth it."

* * *

Two hours into the journey south, Mike became very quiet. He was thinking about the most effective way to tackle another ex-cop. He asked

Phil what photo ID he was carrying.

"Driving licence, uni pass..." Phil took his wallet out of his jacket inner pocket.

"Put that sumwhere safer when we get to London, heh?" said Mike.

Phil was about to remind Mike that he was big enough to think for himself, but he managed not to. *Two years on and he's still offering advice about crime prevention*, he thought fondly. He went through the wallet's contents instead.

"Let's look at that one," said Mike, pointing.

"It's from a seminar I attended in Cardiff last month," Phil explained. "On the application of graphemes. I should have handed the pass back in, but for some reason, I didn't."

"I'm glad you didn't. It'll come in handy. 'Philip Hywel Roberts'. Good Welsh name. Can you do a Welsh accent?"

"Don't be daft. My parents might have come from 'the Valleys', but I grew up in Newcastle. You know that."

"Aye. I just wondered."

"Why? What's going on in that devious mind of yours? You're worrying me."

"Well, accordin' to Flaxby, this King bastard's not at work today. If he's out and we've got to wait, then we wait, but I'm thinkin' of ways to find out if he's sittin' at home watchin' the telly, and if he's at home, if he's alone."

"And if he is, then what? You pay him a courtesy call like you did last year when you sorted Daniel Bayliss out?"

Bayliss had accused Phil of unprofessional conduct—until Mike had paid an unofficial visit to his flat.

Mike didn't answer. Dealing with Bayliss had been easy. Charles King had been in the Force.

It wouldn't be as simple to twist an ex-cop's arm up his back.

"Mike…?" said Phil, breaking the silence. "Why are *we* dealing with this anyway? I mean, why didn't Clive just contact Kent police?"

"I can give you one reason. So, they send a couple of uniforms over. Can he accompany them to the station to help with an enquiry about a missing person? He's ex-cop. He knows his rights. He'll claim he doesn't know a thing. Hundreds of people have a dog tattoo. It's pure coincidence he works for a firm that has a fleet of Mercs. He has an alibi for the whole of Saturday. Eventually, they have to let him go. And the shiters who've got Raith react accordingly."

"But they're going to get alerted anyway if *we* do something."

"That depends."

"Mike?"

"I need to think about it."

"But surely Clive's not suggesting that you go in there and beat the guy up? Is he? I mean…"

"Clive hasn't suggested anythin'. All he's done is pass on information. What did you think we were goin' to do, Phil? Knock on the bastard's door and politely ask him to tell us where Raith is?"

Phil sighed.

"Clive tells Kent police, it takes forever. He tells us, it might go sumwhere fast. This is Raith we're talkin' about. You know? Raith? The man you love? We love. For God's sake!"

Phil nodded. He wasn't happy though.

"So the plan is what? Why do I need the ID?"

"So that you can pretend to be doin' a door-to-door survey."

"Great! And what's Plan B?"

"I don't have a proper Plan A yet. Like I said,

I'm thinkin' about it. You were happy enough when, as you say, I sorted Daniel Bayliss out. It's okay if I get my hands dirty, is it? Less okay if you're roped in to help?"

"No! I'm just bothered that if we mess up—if *we* mess up—Raith will be even worse off."

"Okay. I'm sorry. I shouldn't have said that. Positive thinkin' heh? Raith'll be all right." Raith *had* to be all right. "What was this King's postcode? You said you've got it."

Phil read the postcode out, and Mike typed the location into his Street View app. They looked at the screen together.

"Residential. Sixties or seventies lookin' semis. Small gardens. Back alley. See?"

Phil nodded.

"Is that good? It looks quite densely populated. Doesn't that mean there'd be lots of nosey neighbours?"

"Well, even if there are, it doesn't mean much. The ones who see what goes on are often the least likely to do anythin' about it."

"Because they don't want it known that they're nosey?"

"Exactly. Walls probably thin as plasterboard, though, which is a bind. On the other hand…"

"On the other hand, what?"

"Chances are that the back door'll be insubstantial enough to put me foot into."

"Put your foot through the door?!"

"Well, I certainly wouldn't be usin' me shoulder. It's a while since I've bust a door in."

"And what exactly will I be doing while you're demolishing the man's house?"

"You'll be askin' him the survey questions at the front door."

"Oh, God. And to think I should be in Venezuela.

Venez-fucking-uela. Three thousand bloody miles away from here."

"Aah, Phil… I'm so sorry. Your head must be burstin' with all this…"

"Oh, I don't know what my head's doing. This kind of thing—dealing with criminals, creeps like Bayliss and this Charles King and all the other people involved—it sounds daft, but you sort of come alive when you're on a chase. It's how you were last year when we were dealing with those bastards who were trafficking. You'll always be a cop, Mike. In your head, you'll always be a cop."

Mike didn't answer straight away. He thought about the truth of what Phil said.

"Aye. You're right, I suppose, but… I don't miss it the way I did at first. Livin' with you three, I seem to still find myself chasin' low-life, but without all the hassle from the likes of Ron Fortune, and without all the paperwork… all the draggy things about bein' CID. I know what you mean, though. I do enjoy a chase. You're right. Even though the reasons for chasin' are crap. But I'd rather have no chase at all than have this business with Raith. Or that business last year with you. You know that."

"Of course I do."

Mike returned to looking at his phone apps.

Phil stared out at the passing countryside. For a while, the man beside him filled his thoughts, not Raith. A question he'd never asked himself suddenly entered his mind. Could Mike kill? Not for what most people called passion, but for love?

Love and passion. They were embodied in their tattooed hearts, but all four men knew that love and passion were different. Passion was sex. That all-encompassing physical craving when another man kissed you, explored you and allowed you to enter his personal space in the way that only two men fucking each other allow. *This*, in contrast, was the love that held the four of them together, and Mike demanded love, without even realising.

Phil smiled ruefully at his own choice of words: Mike demanded love. *He's magnetic*. *He draws you in*. A tough, hard man, a dozen years a cop. A tough, hard man who was still loyally, tenderly placing flowers on the grave of his first lover. A man who had moved to Tunhead because of the grave! Someone who could contemplate kicking in a back door and fighting… to what? To the death? Because of love of another. Because of Raith. And Mike did love Raith. Of that, Phil had no doubt whatsoever.

They were two twos—he and Raith, Mike and Ross—but they were two twos within a four. They lived together, talked together, laughed, cried and, Ross apart, fucked together. They would do anything for each other. *We're like polyamorous musketeers*, thought Phil. *We'll probably all die together.*

The thought returned him to reality. They were doing this because Raith's life might be in danger. He couldn't allow himself to think that Raith might already be dead. There wouldn't be muskets and swords…

"There'll be knives," he said, as Mike pressed 'Send' on a text to Ross.

"Knives?"

"Back doors lead into kitchens. Kitchens have knives."

"So?"

"Well you haven't any backup."

"I've got backup."

"Me?"

"You use knives."

"Yes—in the operating theatre."

"Same difference."

"Mike! Don't joke. You're not making me feel any better!"

The grey-green eyes that Raith had often despaired of painting were totally serious now.

"Every time I went on duty," Mike said, "I knew what I might be takin' on—shites with sawn-off shotguns, sad cases out of their head with dope, idiots wieldin' bottles of acid. Axes and hammers and plenty of knives. I've seen 'em all. And it didn't stop me turnin' up for work each day. I never thought I was better than them. I never thought that I could outwit them or outfight them or out anythin' them. I just knew that I would do what I could, and if it wasn't enough, then I'd get hurt. If I was willin' to get hurt for people who were strangers, how do you think I feel about gettin' hurt for Raith? I'm willin' to get hurt for Raith. More than willin'. They hurt Raith. They hurt us."

Phil nodded. He understood exactly what Mike meant. His musketeers analogy was right.

Mike squeezed his hand and kept hold of it for the rest of the journey.

Chapter 9

The Edinburgh train was a long one with several carriages. Mike and Ross walked through to the front well before the terminus at London's King's Cross. They were almost the first travellers through the barriers, and then they raced across the road to St Pancras station, opposite, thankful that the crossing lights were green.

South Eastern Trains—which platform? Eleven. A train was due to leave within five minutes.

They dodged between trolleys, luggage, prams and people, and ran up the escalator.

To Phil's surprise, Mike didn't try to sidestep a woman who was standing by the gate, barring their way.

"Thanks," he said as, mutually confirming names, he took a folder off her. There was hardly time to say goodbye, and no time for Phil to ask what was going on. The train left on time, and a quarter of an hour after sitting down, he and Mike were en route to Ebbsfleet International, the second stop along on the high-speed line.

"The folder?"

"That's your questionnaire," said Mike, passing the folder to Phil.

Phil scanned the contents—a slightly amended version of questions asked of the public when a plan to amalgamate aspects of Durham and

Warbridge hospitals had been suggested.

"I don't know what to say!" Phil said.

"Make sure you ask question eight. It's designed to get info about how many people live at forty-three and either side. King lives at forty-three."

Question eight wasn't part of the original survey: "Do you think it will be all right to knock next door? I can come back later if there are people on night shift." According to Clive Flaxby, Charles King was single, married but divorced. He'd kept the house. With luck, he'd still be living on his own.

"If people say 'he', we're fine," Mike explained. "If they say 'they', we might not be. I can't imagine that the people in the street will be into gender-neutral pronouns."

"Me neither. How on earth did you get this stuff?" asked Phil.

"Texted Ross. He wrote it, emailed it to his friend, Melissa, and she forwarded the email to the lady you saw at St Pancras. This Melissa is meetin' us at Ebbsfleet, so she couldn't be in two places at once."

"No wonder you called Ross a little genius."

"Aye, well. Mustn't let him get too big headed, but it's child's play to Ross. I mean, BOTWAC, the Gateshead gallery, all our legal stuff and finances… he's a clever boy. He thought you'd feel easier about askin' things if it was sumthin' you knew about, so he dragged this off the computer. And, also, people like to talk about their health. And if you put that Cardiff ID stuff in this pouch…"

The train drew in, and the two men got out. A lady in a bright red coat was waving at them.

"Melissa?" said Phil as they approached her.

She smiled.

"You must be Phil," she said, "and you must be Mike." Given that Mike was still wearing leathers, it was obvious who was who.

She walked quickly with them to her car. Ross had arranged for them to borrow it.

"Here are the keys," she told them. "My details are in one of the door pockets, should you need to contact me. The sat-nav is set to the man's address. The petrol tank is full. The other things you wanted are in the box on the backseat."

Phil wasn't sure what she meant by 'other things'.

"I've met Raith a few times," she added. "I hope you find him soon."

"Thank you," said Phil, "and thank you so much for all your help. Not just with all this." He pointed to the car. "With making Ross aware that there were problems with the painting."

"No need. Ross is an old friend."

"How will you get home?" asked Mike. "We've got your car."

"Bus to Bluewater. It's just five minutes away. Lots of lovely shops—the biggest arcade in England, I think. Then another bus to Sevenoaks when I've nearly run out of money. Go on. Shoo! Ross said you would be tight on time."

They didn't need to be told twice. They got in the car and left.

Phil drove.

"Kind lady," he said, "and I don't believe for one minute she's going shopping."

"Me neither," said Mike, a little absently. He was still turning over in his mind how he'd tackle a meeting with another ex-cop. If Charles King was at home, of course. If he wasn't then they'd wait. They drove the rest of the way in silence.

Their destination, New Ash Green, was only

minutes from the station. They drove past the house and parked at the end of the street.

"You need to go to several of the houses opposite forty-three," Mike said. "That will look more natural, and it'll give me time to go round the back and recce. Phone me when you get to forty-three and don't ring off. I need to know that you're talkin' to the guy at the front door."

"Why don't you just come to the front door too? Why round the back? Surely that would be easier than having to break in?"

"Easier, but… I don't necessarily expect people to be lookin' out their windows, but if it's just you goin' from house to house, we won't draw attention to ourselves. I'm in bike gear. I'm a bit more obvious, aren't I? The kids'll be at school. October—I don't expect people to be doin' their front gardens… You on your own should be fine."

"What if he just shuts the door in my face? No cold callers, et cetera."

"As soon as the door opens, say you're from Kent County Council and show the ID. People might shut the door to people toutin' for business, but not to the council."

"What if he recognises me, Mike? He must have known what Raith looks like. He might have seen a photo of the two of us together."

"I know, but that's not goin' to happen instantly, is it? He's not goin' to expect you to turn up at his door, and as soon as I hear you talkin' to him, I'll be over that back fence and inside that house, I promise. Or at least makin' so much racket that he'll open the back door himself. He won't have time to make the link. He'll be racin' through to see what's happenin' out the back. Just make sure that you get in as well. Barge in. Fall in! But get in and get the front door shut."

"And then what?"

"Then, one way or another, we find out what's happenin' to Raith."

* * *

An unexpected day off. Great. Charles King lay in bed and didn't get up until late morning, when he dressed and went downstairs. The kitchen stank of last night's Chinese. He shoved the foil and cartons into a bag then opened the back door and put the bag in the bin.

God, the back garden was a mess.

He'd have a coffee, catch up on some TV series that he'd missed and then get out there in the back and do a bit of tidying.

He performed a little cosmetic surgery on a few potted plants that had gone over, gave an end-of-year mow to the patch of grass and dandelion leaves that counted as a lawn, and went back in the house to watch another episode of *Game of Thrones* and drink another coffee. He didn't lock the back door; he intended to go back out.

He was finishing the coffee when the doorbell rang. King answered. No recognition, but there wasn't really time for that. The surprise on the caller's face made King turn sharply round.

"What the—"

A well-aimed kick knocked breath and coffee out of him and sent him to his knees. With eyes screwed up in agony, he could only struggle slightly as he was dragged into the living room and handcuffed to the table leg. A sharp pain in his neck forced his eyes open.

Mike stood well out of the reach of thrashing legs and yanked again on the rope he'd slipped over King's head. King lunged as far as he could towards Mike to gain some slack, but Mike simply stepped a little further away and yanked again. Despite himself, Phil looked aghast—the man was choking.

"Keep fuckin' still," said Mike, emphasising each of the words.

Sensibly, King did as he was told.

"You and some other shite drove down here with Raith Balan on Saturday. Tell us where Raith is."

"I don't know."

Yank.

"I don't know!"

"I'm quite happy to pull this so tight that your eyes'll pop out of your fuckin' head. If I have to, I'll string you up on whatever piece of wall or ceilin' I think'll take your weight. We'll be the last people you see."

Questions, and some answers, raced round Charles King's head. Who were these men? Who was this one? Would he do it? Yes, by the looks of him. What if his boss found out he'd grassed, though?

Better to deal with the here and now and think about the future later.

"He's at a house near Cobham. In a back room."

"How many people are there?" Mike asked that, and other questions. When he was satisfied that King had furnished all the information that they needed, Mike told Phil to phone home and relay it all. "Don't use names. We'll stay here until we know Raith's safe. If you've lied to us," he said to King, "I'll kill you."

A long hour later, Phil's phone buzzed. He read the text.

"He's safe," he said, and walked quickly into the hall.

* * *

The police would take Raith to a local hospital to be checked over, and they would take Raith's statement. Mike had to keep his own, Phil's and Clive Flaxby's names out of all discussions about tip-offs.

He kicked the living room door shut.

"Now what?" said King.

"I ought to beat you to fuckin' pulp for what you did," said Mike, "but I don't need to, do I? When you get sent down for your part in all this, your cellmates'll do it for me. Ex-cop? They'll love that. And when you come out, your boss'll have his friends waitin' cos you grassed him up. You'll probably wish you were back inside."

King didn't speak. He'd been thinking the same thing for the last half hour.

"I'll do a deal with you," Mike continued. "You keep quiet about this visit. We'll keep quiet about you—long enough for you to make yourself scarce that is. Your name 'll come up—it's bound to—but if you've got any sense, you'll be long gone by then."

King gave a single nod. Mike opened the door, still making sure he was nowhere near King's feet. Phil was sitting on the stairs, his face hidden by his hands.

"Phil," said Mike, "put this shite's details in a text, but only send it if he tries anythin' stupid."

Phil came back into the room, looking puzzled, but did as he was told. Mike removed the rope around King's neck. Then he removed the handcuffs.

"Fucking shite!" said King as he realised what

Mike had just done. Joke handcuffs. He shook his head at his own stupidity.

Phil left first. When he and his mobile were safely out of the house, Mike left too, and an hour later, so did Charles King.

* * *

Mike and Phil walked back to the car.

"Can you drive?" Phil asked. "I'm... I don't know what I am."

Mike looked at the size of the pedals. "Not in these boots," he said. "Swap shoes and I will."

Phil took off his shoes but didn't bother to replace them with Mike's biker boots. He sat in the passenger seat.

"Would you have killed him?" he asked quietly.

Mike met his gaze squarely. "No. I'd like to think that I would've. For you. For Ross. For Raith. But, no. Not like that. In a fight, aye, maybe, but not like that."

"I'm glad." Phil managed a slight smile. "I suppose we can't see Raith yet, can we? We're not meant to be down here, are we? That's why you let King go, isn't it?"

"No. No. Exactly. Come on. Let's get this car back to Melissa and then give it an hour or two, and we'll go and see Raith."

"He's still not safe, is he? I mean, from what that bastard, King, was saying, his boss is worrying about people who are a few points higher on the nasty scale."

Mike nodded. "We know more than we did, though, Phil. One step at a time, heh? The important thing is we've got him back." He squeezed Phil's thigh affectionately and started the car.

A few hours later, Phil held a subdued, bruised, dishevelled Raith tightly in his arms.

* * *

The three men checked into a Holiday Inn. Raith lay unwinding in the bath while Mike went shopping for clean clothes.

A little later, Phil sat on the bed, with Raith, still very quiet, tucked under his elbow.

"We can easily fit three in this," Phil said to Mike. "It's big enough."

"No. I'll stay next door," said Mike. "I'm ready to sleep." He bent down and hugged and kissed Phil, turning him aside so Raith wouldn't see Phil's tears. "Be brave," he whispered. Crying was fine, but probably not just then. "Come here, you!" he told Raith. "Love you, you fuckin' idiot." He hugged and kissed him. Then he went quickly out of the room, knowing that, if he'd stayed, he'd have shed a few tears too.

"I want to stay awake all night," said Raith. "I just want to know I've got you and you've got me. I was scared, Phil. I was angry, but then I was scared."

"I know, love."

"Will you hold me tight, Phil, and kiss me, and—Phil!"

"What?"

"I've still got a piece of fucking crayon up my ass! The bath water sort of melted it a bit."

"What?!"

In the room next door, Mike was puzzled. Given that his shopping expedition had included buying a tube of lube, he'd half expected to hear creaking bed springs. Maybe groans and moans.

But squealing and giggling? He smiled, yawned, and five minutes later he was fast asleep.

* * *

Phil and Raith took their breakfast in their room. Mike had his in the restaurant then knocked on their door. He was pleased to see Raith propped up in bed enjoying a tub of yoghurt.

"It's toffee," Raith said by way of a greeting. "Try some." He offered Mike a spoonful.

"No thanks. Mornin'." He exchanged a knowing look with Phil. "We need to get back ASAP."

"Give me a chance. I've hardly eaten for three days," Raith complained. "Can I have your croissant, Phil?" He took it before Phil could object. "What do you expect me to wear, anyway?" he said, reaching for a pat of butter.

"Those," said Mike, pointing to the clothes he'd bought the previous evening. "Socks, pants, Ts and a jacket. There's nuthin' wrong with 'em."

"There is if you're me."

"Thank you for goin' shoppin' on my behalf, Mike. It was very kind of you," Mike said sarcastically. "He doesn't improve, does he?"

Phil just smiled.

Mike tutted. "If you feel they're insufficiently designer for your image, you can bloody travel in the nuddy."

"I'll catch a cold if I do that!"

"You won't even catch the train if you don't get a move on. Stop bloody whinin'."

Very pointedly and very slowly, Raith began spreading butter on the croissant.

"Move it! Half an hour at most!" Mike said and returned to wait in his own room.

Three-quarters of an hour later, they were handing in their room keys.

Seven hours later, they were stepping off the train at Warbridge. Ross was needed at the gallery in Gateshead, but he'd arranged for one of the BOTWACers to collect Phil and Raith and ferry them home. Mike changed back into his leathers in the IAM office and picked up his bike. He roared past them on the Tun Beck lane, fast and flying.

'Fast and flying' was the motto stencilled in gold on his jacket. It was a description of the way he liked to ride, and a play on Raith's rendition of his surname. *"You're an angel not an angle,"* Raith insisted.

That evening, everything that had happened finally felt real.

The four men had been relaxing in their living room with films and bottles of beer. Raith went into the kitchen to fetch more brown ale for himself and Phil. There was the sound of glass breaking, followed by banging and shouting.

Phil was first to the kitchen. Raith was banging a bottle over and over against the kitchen wall. Beer trickled down the wall. Blood trickled down Raith's wrist.

"Hey, hey," Phil said soothingly. He grabbed a tea towel and gently but firmly prised the broken bottle out of Raith's fingers. "You don't need to do that," he said in the same calm tone. "Shh, now."

"But they'll kill me," said Raith. "Not the ones who kidnapped me. The ones they're scared of. They'll do like in those photographs, and they were horrible, and I don't want people treating me like that, and I don't know what to do, and I wish I'd never painted anything in my life, and I wish I wasn't this fucking tetra thing! Phil!"

"Hey, now. Let's sort this cut out, and then we'll all talk about it."

"Talking won't help, though."

"It always helps. You know that's how we deal with things." Phil led Raith to the sink, and Raith let Phil clean the cut and bandage it. "See. Expertly done." Phil gave Raith's hand a little kiss.

Despite his fears, Raith smiled.

And so they talked, reminding Raith that they knew a great deal more about the situation now than they had two days ago, and encouraging him by repeating that whoever 'they' were, they weren't aware that there was anything wrong with the paintings bought from Danik Amelin, and that, anyway, the paintings might be genuine. Most importantly, 'they' didn't know of Raith's involvement. The four men knew something else too. Flaxby had told them who the grass was within the Tyneside crew.

He'd phoned Mike an hour or so earlier. The feeling was that Danik Amelin was punching well above his weight. Abduction and intimidation weren't the usual ways he ran his business affairs. The fact remained that Raith had been kidnapped, and kidnapping was an indictable offence.

"He'll plead guilty," Flaxby had said. "His lawyers have told him that, even with good character, it's eight years otherwise, especially as he allowed his minions to rough Raith up a little bit. No sign of Charles King, though. Do you know anything about that?"

"I don't know where he is," said Mike.

"Mm. That wasn't exactly what I asked you."

Mike remained silent. Best that Flaxby didn't know anything at all of his deal with King, especially as the deal was done to keep the super's name well out of things.

"The other business… Who tipped Amelin off? Amelin isn't fingering anyone, but I think I know who pointed him in Raith's direction. Charles King was stationed in Maidstone in Kent when he did his two years in the Force. That was Anthony Rybak's division before he transferred to the Met. The two men knew each other."

"Fuckin' hell."

"Now look, Mike. Before you go jumping to any conclusions, he might have tipped King off unwittingly—a simple discussion of the case."

"He shouldn't have been doin' that."

"I know, but we all do it. There's nothing in his record to suggest he's bent, so be careful. Don't go making accusations you can't support with evidence."

Flaxby couldn't see Mike's face, but he could imagine the look on it from the huff of disgust that travelled to his ear.

"I know. Okay, I take that back. You always did sew your cases up more tightly than anyone I've ever known. But be careful, eh?"

"Aye. Thanks Clive."

"I'll keep you informed."

Flaxby disconnected.

Once all that was explained to Raith, he looked much calmer. He examined his bandaged hand.

"You've made a nice job of that, Phil," he said seriously.

"Oh, good." Phil smothered a smile.

Raith sighed. "I'll sweep the broken glass up in the morning," he promised.

"All done while Phil was cleaning you up," said Ross. "Don't worry."

"And it will be all right?"

"The kitchen?"

"No. Me. Well, me and us, mura… mura…"

"Murologically speaking?"

"Yes."

"Strong walls, love. Nothing will break them," said Ross firmly.

'Murology' was a word that Ross had coined himself. He said that their quad had strong walls held together by a mortar of love, passion, honesty and openness. 'Murology'—the study of walls.

Raith nodded, and yawned.

"Why don't we get to bed?" Phil suggested. "And tomorrow we'll get on with sorting all this out."

More nods were followed by goodnight kisses, and Phil gently guided Raith out of the room and up the stairs.

"We ought to get up, too," said Ross.

"Yeah." Mike was still standing but didn't seem ready to make a move.

"Are you overthinking or are you overtired?"

"Bit of both. It's been a hectic few days."

Ross patted the vacant seat next to him and firmly said, "Sit down."

Mike sat down next to him, and Ross entwined his fingers round Mike's left hand. It was his age-old way of encouraging Mike to say whatever was on his mind.

After a minute, Mike began to explain. "Phil was worried that I might kill Charles King."

"Kill him?"

"Mm. I had a noose round his neck. To scare him, but Phil asked me if I would've killed him. Retribution."

"But you didn't."

"No, I didn't. Why wasn't I angry enough? I think the world of Raith, but I didn't even beat the fucker up. Does that mean I don't care about Raith as much as I thought I did? Do you see what I'm sayin'?"

"Yes, I think so. You feel that love for Raith should have caused you to act more violently."

"More... emotionally, and then maybe more violently."

"And did Phil react violently?"

"No, not at all. I think he was glad I didn't."

"What about emotionally?"

"Not in the way I mean, no."

"So, if Phil didn't want the guy strangled to death, why does it bother you that you didn't?"

"I know, but... Phil and I are different."

There was a pause while Ross considered the best way to deal with Mike's feelings.

"Well, tell me how you think of Raith," he said after a while.

"I... he... I think he's fuckin' sexy. I love his eyes, his hair, the shape and the smell of the man. I love the way he makes love. It hurts when he tops, but I don't mind. It makes it intense. You tell me his pictures are great—well, maybe they are, but I'm no connoisseur and I don't see it. His ceramics, though. I can see they're sumthin' else. How he can put what we have in the bedroom into a lump of clay... I don't know, but he does. I get a hard-on just lookin' at them."

"Well, thinking of the heart in our tattoos, that's the passion part isn't it? The sex, but I was thinking more of the kind of love that isn't all about sex and passion. I mean, I love Raith, but not in a sensual, erotic way. More as... family, I suppose. Not as a brother, or a son but, in a sense, like family."

"Well if my brother had been like Raith, I *would* 'ave killed someone by now. The man's got a screw loose, but it's not a problem, I suppose. He'd win prizes if they were dished out for moanin', but I just let that wash over me. I know it's comin' from this mixed-up mess inside his head, and I know that he's confused and bewildered. I think that bein' Raith must be very hard."

"So do I."

"And, aye, family is one way to describe it. In the sense that it's much closer than a friendship. It certainly felt like family before we knocked the two houses through—all yellin' at each other to get out of the bloody bathroom in the mornin'. Put me in mind of growin' up in Bishop and havin' three ruddy sisters! It doesn't describe it properly, though. I mean, family to Phil can't be anythin' wonderful, so I doubt if he'd see Raith like that. But what's botherin' me, Ross, is what's behind the way I act? Is it for Raith, because I love him and want to protect him, or is it for me, because I want the quad? Do you see what I mean?"

"Yes. Do you act altruistically or selfishly?"

"Mm."

"Is it important for you to know?"

"I don't know. I think so."

"Well, I'm not trying to skate over the problem, but I think it's probably both. Not in the sense of six of one and half a dozen of the other. I mean that one… begets the other and they're so closely interlinked that it's pointless trying to prise them apart."

Ross let Mike's hand go and, instead, placed his hands on Mike's cheeks, turning his head so they looked at each other.

"Perhaps love isn't so much a question of whether you would or you wouldn't harm someone who hurts the people and things you care about, but whether you would harm yourself," Ross said. "That's the ultimate proof of love, isn't it?

Self-sacrifice. And you were willing to sacrifice yourself for me two years ago. Your career, your self-respect, your life."

"I'd do it again. You know I would," Mike said quietly.

"I know." Ross took Mike's hand again. "Would you do it for Raith?"

Mike sighed. "Would I do it for Raith?" he echoed. "I don't know. It's hard to imagine how you'd act until you're in that place where you have to choose."

"You did the right thing when you were down south yesterday, Mike. The amount and kind of love you have for Raith wasn't part of that particular scenario. It wasn't a situation where you had to make that choice. You don't have to ask yourself questions or beat yourself up about what you did or didn't do, or about what it signifies." Ross spoke with finality.

Mike nodded.

"Come on," said Ross. "Let's go up."

Chapter 10

The police were right in their assessment of Danik Amelin. Roughing people up wasn't the usual way he ran his affairs.

Pryce and Amelin Associates: architects and civil engineers. They saw projects through from initial design (Amelin) to completion (Leo Pryce), and their work was top notch and very highly thought of. The problem was, so was that of several competitors. Several years before, Pryce had thought of a solution: "We offer kickbacks," he'd suggested. "We only have to fund the first deal. Then it pays for itself." The strategy was successful. They offered individuals under-the-table payments to send work their way even though their charges were far higher than anyone else's. The high charges paid for the next deal. They'd felt the need to hire two or three men who were willing to double as heavies—Charles King was one, and the driver of the Merc another—just in case the competition learnt about their business style and took exception to it, but there was never any quarrel with the standard of their work. It was completed efficiently and professionally. Their reputation steadily grew and brought them into contact with a man called James Lennard.

In some ways, Lennard and Danik Amelin could have been brothers. They shared several similar traits: they liked good food and drink, they had a fondness for eye-catching architecture and they collected paintings. Like brothers, though, they had their differences. Amelin collected works of art primarily because he enjoyed looking at the canvasses; he appreciated the skill behind the execution. Lennard only appreciated the ease with which he could sink ill-gotten gains behind a facade of legal transactions. The way he amassed those ill-gotten gains indicated a further difference between the two.

Amelin, whose firm had lucrative contracts in every continent except Antarctica, knew he sometimes had to bend the law—a little pressure here and there to encourage the competition to withdraw its tender. Lennard didn't simply bend the law. He broke it, and broke people when they crossed him. He hadn't been responsible for the photographs that frightened Raith, but he could have been. He adopted a 'no holds barred' attitude to business. No orifice was safe, and when he'd dealt with the holes, he started on the bones. At least, that was his method if people had information that he wanted. If it was simply a case of somebody getting in his way, he'd tie their hands and feet and dump them out of his yacht or private plane. Or so people said.

Danik Amelin had heard the rumours. He didn't want to test their accuracy. He didn't want to contact Lennard and suggest that the two Ivashova paintings he'd sold him were fakes if they weren't. That was why he had kidnapped Raith—to find out. If Raith had confessed, he'd have known where he stood and what he'd have to do, but now he was even worse off. On bail, yes, with a trial looming over him. Perhaps, by then, the fraudster, be it Raith or someone else, would have been found. He knew the police were still involved. There was no reason why Lennard should even learn of the situation, not with the spin that the police were putting on the crime. The official line was that Raith had been kidnapped for ransom money. But Amelin knew he was kidding himself. If Lennard should learn of a question mark over the paintings, and that he hadn't admitted that he was aware of it...

He picked up his phone and, nervously, dialled.

* * *

Nick Seabrooke discussed the rationale behind the official line when he visited the quad on the Thursday. The hope was that another fake Ivashova might surface, and with people in the know alerted, its provenance might be quickly traceable.

"But that assumes that no middle man, or woman, is involved," said Ross. "I don't mean to cast aspersions on gallery owners—I mean, I'm one—but if there's someone out there who is knowingly involved in this, it just tells them to sit tight."

"No, Ross, no general alert, for the very reason you've just given, but we have our contacts."

"You can say that again," said Raith, accusingly. "Your fucking contacts got me kidnapped."

Anthony Rybak had been taken off the case and suspended on full pay, pending an investigation.

"And I can't work 'til my hand is better," Raith complained.

"You call makin' erotic shapes out of lumps of clay 'work' do you?"

The two-finger sign that Raith gave Mike stretched his damaged skin. "Ow!"

"Serves you right," said Mike.

Raith repeated the gesture with the fingers of his other hand.

* * *

For the second time, polyam-related thoughts were on Nick Seabrooke's mind as he drove back to base. He enjoyed being with the quad. Ross's friendly chatter, Mike's good-humoured teasing—which, Nick noticed, the others countered with retorts of their own if they felt Mike overstepped the PC mark—Phil's quiet seriousness, even Raith's moaning... there was something relaxing and endearing about it all. Again, he asked himself what he had expected. That they would be constantly kissing or, revolting thought, waggling pricks at each other? He chided himself. Homophobia *and* polyphobia! Well, if they got personal with each other, they clearly did so in private, not when visitors were around.

Nick didn't have to separate the public from the private. Occasionally, he went to meets, but the nature of his job meant that he had to choose his friends, even if that's all they were, with care. He enjoyed his job. It didn't bother him that life was work, work, work, and yet... each time he'd driven away from Cromarty, he'd had a feeling that something filled the air in that little house in Tunhead that made him envious. Was there something missing from his life? Companionship maybe? It wasn't exactly that.

"If I had to put a name on it," he told himself, "I suppose I'd call it love."

He'd never experienced love. Not really. Not love that was reciprocated. He'd had crushes—

or possibly, squishes: 'crushes' sounded too romantic, 'squishes' too platonic. There'd been a guy he'd fancied once, years previously, when he'd first started uni. That was when he'd decided that he wasn't, as he'd thought he might be, gay. He'd liked being with his friend, as he called him. He enjoyed his company.

Seabrooke was a Londoner by birth and knew his way around all the capital's places of interest. The friend was from the provinces and pleased to have a guide. All had gone well until—he still cringed with embarrassment when he thought about it—his friend had asked him, "When are we going to do it, then?"

He, being a naïve idiot, had thought the friend was referring to an assignment a tutor had set. He remembered the scene in inglorious detail. He'd said, "But it doesn't have to be in until next week," and his friend had said, "I don't know what you're talking about, but it isn't the same as I am. You know?" And with a sinking heart, he'd realised that he did know.

He'd tried to explain, but even to him it had sounded ridiculous.

"I could probably hug you and give you a cuddle, and I really like you... love you a lot, but I don't want to kiss you or lie with you naked, and I definitely don't want sex."

"You love me, but no fucking?"

"No fucking. No deep kissing. No naked bodies pressed together underneath the sheets."

"That's weird. Love without sex? And what am I supposed to do when I get a hard-on? Wank? Go cottaging? Find a rent boy? Well?"

"I don't know."

"Well, call me when you come up with an answer."

They hardly spoke for the remainder of their

three-year course. Then Nick had learnt of asexuality, and some of how he felt had started to make sense.

He parked the car. He had no doubt that he was totally ace, but where was he on the romantic-aromantic spectrum? Puzzled and somewhat disconcerted, he wondered why he felt the need to ask the question.

* * *

It was a cold, rain-filled, miserable autumn day. Ross was in Gateshead, Phil in Warbridge. Mike had planned to take three bikers out, but one had withdrawn because of the state of the roads. Spray and grease—hardly ideal riding conditions. Mike encouraged the other two to continue the session, and then he began the journey home. Even with wet-weather gear, he was soaked through by the time he reached Tunhead. Unsurprisingly, the place looked deserted. Everyone who normally worked with doors wide open would be staying inside, catching up on paperwork or multi-meal cooking for the freezer; the nearest shop was ten miles away in Tunhope.

Raith's big studio door was shut as well. Mike pushed it open, but Raith was nowhere to be seen. Presumably he was in the house. His car was parked at its usual careless angle, so he obviously hadn't driven anywhere, and Raith wouldn't have gone for a walk if there was a chance of his hair getting wet. He needed to find him—Raith had Cromarty's door key.

"The bloody nuisance," Mike said aloud.

Ross had borrowed Mike's key that morning, having left his own sitting on his desk in the gallery in Gateshead. He'd accidentally left it there the previous afternoon when he'd taken it off the keyring to get to another one on the bunch, and he'd forgotten to replace it.

Raith had intended to work in his studio. He'd promised to let Mike in.

Mike banged on Cromarty's front door. No answer. He looked through the living-room window. No Raith. He went around the back and looked into the kitchen. Raith wasn't there. Raith wasn't the type to have a daytime kip, so chances were he wasn't upstairs either. *Where the fuck is he*? Mike wondered. He returned to the street. *If he's drinkin' tea all nice and warm in someone's house, I'll kill him! I'm fuckin' drenched!* But he had an uneasy feeling.

He stood outside the studio. The tarmacked lane that led to Tunhead gave out just before the houses. Stone blocks hewn from Tunhead quarry made an uneven paving for what became the Street. Mike was staring at the water that trickled down between the slabs, wondering what to do, when he realised that one of the rivulets was streaked with red. Blood? No. Blood would have washed away in all this rain.

He bent down and hooked some whatever-it-was out of a gap between two blocks of limestone. He pressed it between his finger and thumb. It didn't dissolve, yet it felt like powder. A little clump of it was trapped in a hollow a couple of metres further on. Beyond that clump was another. Glaze powder. For a reason he didn't yet understand, Raith was leaving him a trail.

He followed the pockets of powder to the end of the Street. At the top, a flagstone path led to the church and its graveyard on the right. A well-worn grassy track led left, onto the moors, skirting the quarry on its way to Raith's favourite waterfall at Harnell Force. *Which fuckin' way?*

Mike's heart rate started to quicken. He didn't need the red trail anymore. It was obvious that several people had recently trampled down the grass on the moorland track. Out of season, in this weather, they were unlikely to be hikers.

Mike raced along, oblivious now to the rain and the cold and the clothes that stuck to his skin, and then he spotted them—three men and Raith at the bottom of the quarry. Instinctively, he flattened. The men had their backs to him. One had hold of Raith. The other two were standing slightly to the side, and one was armed.

Waves of thought surged and broke in quick succession. Were the others armed? How long would the police take to get here? On any day, too long. On one like this with flooding causing havoc on the six-eight-nine... and anyway, he'd need an armed response not pepper sprays and tasers. That would take even longer. He could ask his friends in the hamlet to help, but that would endanger them and Raith. First rule of policing: keep the public safe. *Shite. I'm not sure what to do.*

Then he made a decision.

Mike wriggled backwards until he was certain he was out of the line of sight, and he raced back to his bike. With a bit of luck, they'd think he was just an off-roader having fun. He'd have to hope that Raith would recognise the bike or the helmet design and get out of the way. He pictured the descent. He knew he could ride, he was good, but his Honda was a street bike. It wasn't built for hurtling down the steep, wet, overgrown side of a quarry. If he came off too soon... Raith was in danger. He'd chance it.

This time, he didn't try to hide. He made sure they heard his engine roar. They looked up. He was already halfway down the quarry side, fast and flying. He jumped off his bike a split second before it ploughed into them.

He rolled and brought down one man while the bike careered into a second one, pinning him to the ground. Raith yelled "Gun!" just as the third man took aim. Mike used the man he was struggling with as body armour. Two bullets lodged in the man's back and, with a grunt, he lost consciousness.

The quarry had long been used as a dumping ground. Raith wrenched a heavy piece of rusted, jagged metal from a heap of scrap behind him and swung it with all the force he had. He gasped when he saw the result—the gunman's wrist was nearly sliced in two. With a howl of pain, he dropped the gun. Raith grabbed it, then stood there, eyes and mouth wide open with horror.

Ten seconds of carnage. Three men badly injured. Two men perfectly safe.

Mike and Raith looked at each other.

"That was exciting," said Raith. Then he turned around and vomited.

Mike pulled his phone out of his jerkin. Smashed.

"Can you walk okay?" he asked when the retching stopped.

Raith nodded.

"Then go back up and phone for the police and an ambulance."

Raith nodded again. "Shall I come back when I've done that?" he asked.

"No. Knock someone up and get them to give you a drink. And ring Phil," he added. "Ask him to come home."

"Will you be all right here? Do you want the gun?"

Mike looked at the three men on the ground. They weren't going to be a problem. He wouldn't have wanted the gun anyway.

"No. Make sure the catch is on."

Raith did so and began to scramble up the quarry side.

Mike crouched beside the man who'd once held the gun and now held his wrist. "Who do you work for?"

The man blanked Mike out, a look Mike recognised, and didn't reply. He might be incapacitated, but he knew how to deal with questions and with pain.

Mike walked over to the bike. The man underneath it was breathing erratically. He looked at Mike imploringly. One leg was clearly broken. Mike kicked it, hard. The man screamed. Mike kicked it again and asked the same question.

"Who do you work for?"

Still no answer. Mike bent over and ground the handlebars further into the man's damaged chest.

"Talk," he said, "or I'll keep twistin'."

After a minute, he got an answer. After an hour, he heard the sound of sirens.

* * *

"Sir? Sir!"

It took Mike a moment to register the fact that a uniformed cop was talking to him. He turned tired eyes in PC Rogers' direction, and recognition flooded in.

"Oh, hi! Sorry, I was miles away."

"Not surprised, sir. Nice to see you, though not

in circumstances like this." The constable waved his arm in an explanatory gesture.

"No." Mike sat there, gazing at two paramedics tugging his mangled bike off an equally mangled man.

"You can go back to your house now, if you want, sir." He followed Mike's gaze. "We'll try and get it up for you."

"There's no need..."

"Well, we'll try. Can't promise."

Mike nodded, unstuck himself from his limestone boulder and slowly made his way home.

Later, in Warbridge station's canteen, PC Rogers told his version of events to an audience comprising people with fond memories of Detective Inspector Angells, and people who were curious about an ex-colleague who wasn't just gay: he was polyamorous!

"It was bedlam," said Rogers. "It's only a tiny place—Tunhead—and there's our lot and the paras and police cars and ambulances everywhere... You've been there, haven't you, Jakes? When we were on that farm ops case a couple of years ago?"

"That's right," PC Jacobs confirmed. "The DI arranged a night watch—us, the farmers and some of the art crowd who live there. The DI's partner, Whitburn, he was okay. Balan was more worried about losin' beauty sleep than catchin' criminals. The fourth one, the doctor, wasn't involved, though I've met him a few times at the hospital."

"Anyway, it was bedlam. The super was there, too. Then, in the middle of all this, there's the sound of a car driven hard, and the doc arrives and screeches to a halt a nail's length from an ambulance. He nearly needed it himself. He races in the house yellin' 'Raith!' and—"

"—so I came racing in," Phil said to Ross that evening, "expecting to find Raith hysterical. I was ready to scoop him up in my arms and try to calm him, and what do I see? Raith sitting by the kitchen radiator like a king receiving tribute, enrobed in a duvet, drinking soup and smiling graciously at this… this queue of BOTWACers carrying plates of cakes and flasks of hot drinks! I was totally floored by his composure."

"Well, the one thing you can say for certain about Raith is that he's unpredictable," said Ross, smiling.

"No. Extremely predictable," said Phil. "If I'm not mistaken, he's going to milk this for all that it's worth. I can see it already." He mimicked a wimpy voice: "Do I have to mop the kitchen floor? I'm still bravely suffering from my ordeal. I don't think I should do my turn on washing up; I still feel very delicate."

"Raith, delicate? Deluded more like it! Well, if he tries that on, I'm going to call him Hansel. Or Gretel. That was pretty clever, though, Phil, grabbing the glaze powder and leaving a trail. You've got to hand him that."

"He probably had a hole in his pocket and it was already there! Trickled out without his knowing. No… I'm being mean, and I'm sure the hysterics will come. At the moment, though, he's still on an adrenaline buzz. I think I am, too."

They heard the toilet flush.

"I'll get him to bed," said Phil. "Will you be okay with Mike?"

"I'll give him another ten minutes and then I'll go after him. I know where he'll be."

* * *

Mike, showered, dry, and looking better for two strong cups of sugary tea, had given his statement to Flaxby several hours earlier.

"It was either me or Ron Fortune," Flaxby had said, "and I figured that you would prefer me."

Mike had offered a tired smile and went on to recount the events.

"I don't know, Mike," said the super when Mike had finished. "The pair of you were very, very lucky."

"I know. You don't have to tell me. What could I do, though?"

"I wish I could say that this will bring us nearer to discovering what's behind all this."

"You agree with me, then. It's not Raith."

"Absolutely. Those three won't talk, though. One of them isn't in any state to, but the other two... they're not going to say a word."

"No, I know."

"The car they arrived in was stolen, by the way. Reported a week ago. False plates."

"Not surprisin'."

"Look, I'm going to make a request."

Mike stopped staring into the distance and wondered what Flaxby was going to say. Leave it to the police, perhaps?

"No, not to you," Flaxby said. "I'm going to see if we can get that painting up here. I'll ask the Chief to contact her opposite number at the Met. Raith's been very lucky twice..."

"Thanks, Clive. I know Ross thinks it might help if Raith actually saw the bloody thing. If we can sumhow get the heat off him..." Mike placed his hands on his eyes and rubbed them. "God, I'm knackered."

"We'll all be out of your hair soon. Get something to eat and get Phil to give you something to combat overtiredness."

"To wake me up?"

"To help you sleep."

"Aye. You know sumthin'? It's… different when it's so close to home. You deal with it when it's your job, but this isn't my job. This is Raith, and I know he's a pain in the ass, but… he's Raith. You know? He's a great guy, really. And it affects Phil and Ross, especially Phil. And it doesn't just affect them, Clive…" He snuffled. There were tears in his eyes. "It affects me and everythin' we've got here. Cos it's so special, what we've got, and I love them, you know. Each of them. Oh, God. I'm sorry. Shit. Blubberin'. Sorry."

Flaxby waited until Mike recovered his self-control. "Don't apologise," he said. "It really isn't necessary."

The police had finally left. Mike had picked at his food. He didn't want anything heavy, just a sandwich, but he didn't really want that either. The rain had stopped. Raith was having a bath before, at Phil's insistence, an early night.

"I need to clear my head," Mike had said. "I'm goin' out for half an hour."

"Do you want me to come too?" asked Ross.

"If you like. I just need to… I don't know… I just need to go out."

Ross had taken that response to mean "not at the moment," rather than a categorical "no," which was why he'd told Phil he would give Mike ten more minutes, then he'd follow.

So, with Phil and Raith in bed, Ross slipped on a jacket and, quietly shutting the front door, made his way to the churchyard. Mike was exactly where Ross had expected him to be, sitting at the side of the grave he always chose to sit beside. Ross walked over and wrapped an arm round Mike's shoulder.

"Thanks," Mike said eventually. "I'm not proud of what I did," he admitted, feeling the need to explain. "I'm no sadist. You know that, but the cops don't dare to touch anybody now. I had to try to find out what was happenin', for Raith's sake."

"I know, love. Stop beating yourself up about it. There's no need."

But Mike continued to try to justify his actions to himself. "It was a case of them or Raith."

"Actually, love, it was a case of you or Raith. What you did was very brave."

"What I did was very bloody stupid. It could've gone either way. Well, I can add it to my little stock of nightmares, along with all the other ones I wreck your sleep with every night."

Mike was someone who dealt efficiently with waking hours but fell apart in sleeping ones. Not because of dreams that stemmed from having been a cop. Memories of people ruled his subconscious mind, not least the memory of the man whose grave he tended.

"Actually, you've been getting better," Ross said. It was true. Years of tender care had helped Mike to deal with his nighttime tears and fears. "It's been my own worries that have kept me awake recently, worries about Raith. Seriously, love, you knew that at least one of those three men was armed. You weren't the one who had information that they wanted. They'd have shot you, and you took that risk."

"Mm. What an irony, hey, Ross? I think I've been in more danger since I left the Force than I ever was while I was in it!" He sucked in a deep breath and let the air out with a long, slow sigh.

Ross stood up. "It's damp. Come back in. Let's get to bed."

Mike nodded. The two men walked home and quietly let themselves in.

"Do you think we can run to a new bike? And new leathers?" asked Mike, once he and Ross had undressed and were tucked up together.

"If you're very good."

"Good like this?"

Mike twisted round and lay on top of Ross. Ross wrapped his legs round Mike's body, in part to lessen Mike's weight.

"Much gooder than that. That won't even get you the leathers."

"Like this then…"

Ross opened his mouth, expecting a tongue. Instead, Mike suddenly rolled off him and lay on his back.

"Can't do it, Ross."

Ross altered his own position and stroked Mike's face.

"If one of my DCs had done to that guy what I did to him… I mean, the guy's leg was broken. God!" A shorter sigh this time. "What a lousy thing to 'ave done."

"Mike."

"Aye?"

"I'm glad you feel bad about it. Not in a critical way, love. Just because it means you care. You've always had a conscience. It's one of your best and worst qualities. Come on. Come here."

Mike turned on his side and let himself be kissed and cuddled and caressed. He gave another sigh. A far more relaxed one this time.

"So, what sort of bike do you fancy?"

There wasn't any answer.

Ross gave Mike a little kiss, even though he knew that Mike, asleep, wouldn't be aware of it.

"You wonderful man," Ross whispered. "Sweet dreams."

* * *

Three hours later, nightmares woke Ross up. Not Mike's. Nor his own. Raith's.

Ross listened to muffled exchanges. He knew that Phil was doing what, so often, he had done with Mike—soothing, encouraging, gently kissing a return to calm. There was a difference, though. Mike's dreams held echoes of the past. Raith's held fears for the future. Ross pulled the covers over his head and tried to shut the future out.

In fact, his assessment wasn't totally right.

"I'm frightened, Phil," said Raith.

"Of course you are, love. It was a very frightening thing to have happened."

"No. I'm not frightened because of what happened. I thought, *Oh, here we go again*, and almost switched off, if that makes sense. I felt sort of calm, somehow. That's why I thought about the powder. Even when Mike came tearing down the side of the quarry, it was like, *Oh, right, the cavalry's here*. It's more..." Raith stroked Phil's wedding ring finger. "It's more that I'm frightened for us. I don't want anything to happen to us and break us up. Me and you, but the four of us, too."

"That's not going to happen, love."

"I'm not stupid, Phil. I know I can act it sometimes, and I know you all sometimes think I'm a screwball, but I'm not stupid in a stupid sense. Mike could have died, couldn't he? The shite with the gun—he tried to shoot him. I'd have felt guilty for the rest of my life if Mike had died. I'd feel awful. I feel guilty about it right now, thinking that I put Mike in danger."

Phil searched for words that would reassure.

"Mike's… different from you and me and Ross," he said. "He was a detective, don't forget. He's faced people with knives and bottles and baseball bats and sawn-off shotguns. He doesn't look for confrontation, but he's willing to meet it head on, if and when it looks for him. It's just the way he is."

"But he's not invincible, is he?" Raith didn't look convinced.

"No. He's not invincible. But he doesn't think he is. He's trained to assess a situation. Assess it quickly and make a decision based on what he sees. He wouldn't have done what he did unless he'd thought he'd be successful." Phil wasn't actually sure if that's what Mike had thought, but he felt he ought to play the risks down.

Raith considered his explanation and looked a little cheerier.

"And he was right, wasn't he?" said Phil, pouncing on the happier look. "You're here, all safe and warm in bed with me, and Mike's here, all safe and warm in bed with Ross."

"Mm. Mike usually is right, isn't he?"

"Yes."

"So you don't think he was in as much danger as I thought?"

"Well, I think he was in danger, but as I said, I think that he would have assessed the situation and he felt he could deal with it. With your help. You played a big part, remember."

That was the wrong thing to say.

"It was like one of those photographs the sergeant brought here, Phil. The guy's hand was hanging off. It was horrible, and it makes me think of when Peri and that shite, Babcock, had Mike that time and hurt his hand."

Peri Lescaut, Raith's long-ago lover, and Luke Babcock, an ex-con with a grudge. They'd hurt more than his hand. It had taken Mike weeks to recover from their cruelty.

"I know, love, but that's all in the past. Right now, we need to think about finding the person behind the painting and, from what Mike and Ross were saying earlier, things are moving forward. And the plans will help to keep you safe, too."

"And Mike?"

"And Mike."

"So we'll all be safe?"

"Safe as houses."

"Can we play that alphabet game to help us go back to sleep?"

"If you like. Do you want to start from J or from A?"

"Why J?"

"It's where we got to last time."

"From A, cos I've got one. Safe as apartments."

"Good one. Safe as bungalows."

"Safe as cottages."

"Safe as… dormobiles."

"They're cars!"

"Yes, but some people live in them."

"I'll let you have dormobiles if you do E as well."

"Mm. Safe as… Can I come back to E?" asked Phil.

"Okay. Shall I do F?"

"Yes."

"Safe as flats."

"I've got an E now. Safe as eyries."

"Eyries?"

"Eagles' nests."

"That's a good one. Still your turn, because I did F."

But by the time Phil had thought of a G, Raith's eyes were closed. There was more than one way to help his lover to get to sleep. Phil turned onto his side, and soon, he was sleeping too.

* * *

As Phil had predicted, 'things' were discussed more fully the following afternoon.

Mike knew Flaxby couldn't station anyone at Tunhead: there was nobody spare. Raith needed guarding somehow, though. So everyone who lived in the hamlet, except Phil and Raith himself, assembled in the little church, and Mike, with the super in attendance, outlined a plan. All the BOTWACers knew Flaxby, by sight if not in person, because of his wife, Dorothy.

"It's not so much a plan of action," Mike said, "but it won't have us all freezin' our socks off at three in the mornin' like happened the other year. We'd like to close Tun Beck Lane above Askill's Farm. Full-width roadblock."

There were several sheep farms off the lane and Askill's was the most northerly of them. There were various questions to answer:

"How could we get out, though? I mean, if the barrier is meant to keep people out, it keeps us in."

"What if there's an emergency?"

"And we've got kids to take to school," said someone else. "How are we going to get them to the school bus stop if we can't use Tun Beck Lane?"

"We've thought of that," Mike said. "We've got

enough four-wheel drives in the village to ensure that everyone has access to one, and several are Landies, so we'd be fine off-road. Whatever the weather," he added, recalling a journey made the previous year with a badly injured Phil in the back. The Landrover had safely got the four men up and down slopes slippery with mud and three days' solid rain. "The Askills have said that we can take the vehicles over the back fields and meet up with their drive. We all helped them out when we mucked in for the farm op three years ago. It's payback time."

There were murmurings as people recalled their involvement in catching a gang of thieves.

"How would we get supplies in, though?" someone asked. "Stuff that won't go into cars?"

Ross spoke. "I'm happy to arrange deliveries up to and from the police's roadblock. Hire a van and keep it on this side. The quad will bear the charge. It means keeping BOTWAC closed at weekends, but at this time of year, we don't get many visitors anyway. And if anybody needs additional insurance to drive the off-roaders, we'll cover that as well. In fact, any extra expenses, or losses, we'll cover them."

"Week*ends* you said, Ross. How long will this go on for?"

"At least a week, and maybe more. Just to give the super here, and us, a chance to work on this without feeling that Raith's in danger all the time. And I've another request. Sorry. The guy who's been leading the fraud investigation is driving up later this evening. We've got spare bedrooms in Cromarty, but… let's say that Raith's a bit delicate at the moment, and if anyone can offer a room—"

"And a few meals without lashin's of chilli pepper," added Mike.

"—we'd be really grateful."

"If he doesn't mind cats on the bed, he can stay with me," someone offered.

"And if he does, we've got a spare," said another BOTWACer.

Mike hadn't felt well all day, and at that point, he sneezed. An hour later, he was using one of Cromarty's spare bedrooms himself. Phil had told him, most forcefully, to go to bed and stay there. He felt too ill to argue.

* * *

Nick Seabrooke was staying in Tunhead for a reason. He'd brought the painting with him, and he didn't want to let it go out of his sight. Raith, Phil and Ross clustered round it.

"It's so small," said Phil with surprise.

Raith's waterfalls were large affairs, at times well over a metre high. They dwarfed the frame held in Raith's gloved hands.

Raith and Ross were more interested in style than size.

"This artist doesn't use a brush like I do," said Raith, looking at a section of the work through Ross's hand lens. "The use of colour is like mine, I can see that, but I wouldn't do that bit like that." He pointed to an area of spray.

"No love, but that's not the point," Ross reminded him. "It's not about how you would approach it exactly, but whether you would be able to copy Masha Ivashova's style of painting. As you've just said yourself, your use of colour is similar."

"I do my own thing, though. I never learnt by copying."

"We know, but that's not exactly the point."

"I know that Mike says that the only words I can spell are swear words, but that doesn't say 'Ivashova', does it?" Raith was referring to the artist's signature. "It says Ubawoba or something. That's a 'U' not an 'I', and they're letter 'b's, but there's no 'b' in her name."

"It's Cyrillic," Ross explained. "Some of the symbols duplicate English ones, but they don't necessarily mean the same."

"So that's an 'I'?" Raith asked, pointing.

"Yes. In cursive. Joined up."

"And what's the ones that look like 'b'?"

"Russian 'v'."

"Oh. Confusing. You know lots of weird stuff."

"Yes. That's what Mike says, too. It comes in useful sometimes."

"Ross was describing the various tests that conservators do to establish authenticity," Phil said. "He said that this painting passed them all, except for the thread count."

"That's right," the sergeant confirmed. "There was no problem with all the basic spectroscopy tests. The canvas wasn't over-painted. Nothing had been retouched. All the pigments that were used would have been available to someone working in that place and at that time, but, as you say, the thread count was wrong."

"Remember what we learnt about Ivashova when we first got wind of this, Phil?" said Ross. "She lived in a little village called Molavanka in northern Russia, and she, or her family, made her frames from local wood. This frame isn't original, by the way, but that's not the point. She always bought her canvas material from the one supplier, and the canvas was always the same in terms of its weave. It seems that there wasn't any choice, just a locally obtainable roll. The warp count on this painting is different from those on her other paintings. It doesn't seem to have been the type of canvas that was normally available. Available to Masha Ivashova, that is."

Raith studied the weave. "It's tighter than I like," he said.

"How did the auctioneers get hold of the comparisons?" asked Phil. "Given that the art world seems to operate on secrecy."

"Very true. It wasn't necessary to make comparisons in person," the sergeant explained. "There are Ivashovas in St Petersburg and Moscow, and in one or two other places. We simply sent the details over."

"The fact that 'our painting' is different from what Ivashova usually used doesn't prove that it isn't hers, though," said Phil.

"That's true as well," Nick said, "but given the sudden influx of this lady's paintings onto the market after several years of silence, it's enough to arouse suspicion. And the fact that our architect friend, Amelin, reacted the way he did suggests that he wasn't entirely convinced of its provenance himself. So, putting together the unusual recent interest in Masha Ivashova and the query regarding the thread count... my lot were contacted."

"Intent to deceive," murmured Phil, echoing a phrase he'd heard Ross use, "but not by Raith." He rubbed Raith's hand affectionately.

"Raith was the obvious suspect," said the sergeant.

"You mean I was the only tetra male you could come up with. Seeing as Ross reckons that fakers are nearly always men. That's sexist, isn't it?"

"I'm afraid it is, Raith."

"But this provenance business," Phil persisted. "What is the story behind the painting? How come you haven't been able to trace the seller, for example?"

"That is one of the two lines of enquiry, Phil. On the one hand, we were looking for a possible artist. Raith."

There was a *hmph* from Raith.

"On the other hand, we're looking at provenance. You're right."

"Well?"

"We've been trying to trace the person who submitted the painting to Lenfitte's. The address that Lenfitte's were given isn't helping. It's a small gallery in Brighton, but between then and now, the lease has run out and the gallery has closed. We're trying to trace the owner, but he's proving illusory. We weren't just trying to pin things on Raith. There are always the two sides of an investigation like this. Find the seller. Find the artist. Often, if we find the first, we find the second. The rest of my crew are working on it. They're not just sitting in London waiting for me to get back. And, obviously, if we find the seller, we can establish some facts about the provenance."

"I didn't mean to put you on the defensive," Phil said apologetically. "It's just that... well..."

"No. I understand."

"I know this is going to sound really stupid," Raith said, "but how does having the painting here help us all find the criminal? Who, we're all agreed, isn't me."

"The painting was sitting in the police's vaults," Ross pointed out. "As Nick has said, various tests were carried out on it, but apparently, not all the possibilities were used. Once it was realised that the thread count was problematic, some of the other tests were put on hold."

"Basically, 'til we'd investigated you lot," the sergeant interrupted.

"To cut a long story short, we're going to use some of the high-tech stuff that Phil has access to in Durham. I'm familiar with the basic principles involved and I've used spectroscopy equipment, but Phil can get his hands on some brilliant stuff from work."

"That's right," Phil said. "Not so much at the hospital, but at the uni... there's everything. Third generation FTIR ..."

"Effty what?"

"Fourier Transform Infra-Red Spectroscopy. We've got it in my department because of the research into grapheme, but the geology department have portable versions. They use it to classify plant fossils, for example. It identifies organic materials, and a mathematical formula converts the data into a spectrum. The spectrum is like a fingerprint."

"Oh."

"It's invasive, in the sense that a tiny bit of original material has to be removed, but you could fit several hundred samples on a pin head."

"What will we be looking for?" asked Raith.

"Tiny clothes fibres stuck under the paint... anything that could tie the work to a place and a time," Ross explained. "Phil will be very handy. He can use a scalpel more accurately than any of us!"

"On bums," Raith reminded them. "Oops. Sorry, Nick."

"No problem," Nick assured him. "For your sake, Raith," he continued, "Superintendent Flaxby arranged for the work to be carried out here, not in London. If this had been a straight case of intent to deceive, there's no way we could have transferred the painting up here. The entire investigation would have been carried out back home. The circumstances are... unusual to say the least."

"For me? Oh. Wow! Did you hear that, Phil? This is cos of me!"

"Yes, Raith."

There was a fit of coughing from upstairs.

"Your patient awakes. And awaits," said Ross to Phil.

"Won't be long," said Phil and left the room.

"It's man flu," Raith asserted.

"Oh yes? Since when have you been a doctor?" asked Ross.

"Well, I got wet too, and I wasn't wearing a crash hat, but I'm not lying in bed being ill, am I?" said Raith, reminding Ross and Nick how wet he'd been.

When Phil returned, a minute or so later, Ross asked, "How is he?"

"Not too good. High temp. Bad colour. Aching all over. I'm hoping it will be a one or two-day thing."

"Raith says it's man flu."

"No. He probably already had a bug, but yesterday took so much out of him that he wasn't able to fight it off."

"Well, I might have already had a bug too," Raith insisted. "I mean, we all live together."

"Yes, Raith. We do, and you might," Phil agreed.

"And my hair was soaking wet. It took an age to dry it." Raith twisted his long ponytail round to remind them that drying his hair took both time and effort.

"Raith, I'm sure that we all recognise that you experienced just as much discomfort as Mike did in the rain, and we're all very impressed by your ability to withstand the onslaught of the influenza virus, but he is poorly." Phil spoke patiently but firmly.

Concerned brown eyes met Phil's stern blue ones. "Very poorly?" asked Raith.

"No. Poorly."

"Sorry," Raith said apologetically.

Phil squeezed Raith's arm to show that no harm was done.

"You can take him a drink if you want to see how he is," he suggested, anticipating the likely answer.

"Well, maybe we just ought to let him rest. Peacefully."

"Yes. That's probably best."

Nick Seabrooke had followed the little Phil and Raith exchanges with interest, and he knew how instrumental Phil had been in securing the transfer of the painting and the access to equipment. He was becoming more aware of the quad's dynamics.

He caught Ross watching him and, well out of Raith's and Phil's lines of vision, they exchanged smiles.

Raith: there were ways he was both younger and older than the other three. Older because he'd learned about life the hard way—in young offenders' wings of overcrowded prisons, in jails where three to a cell was the norm and 'last one in' meant 'first one fucked'.

It wasn't that he was bad. It was more that, as Mike would say, *He's got a bloody screw loose.* It wasn't kind, but it contained a germ of truth: something wasn't wired right. So Raith could be wise and Raith could be foolish. Tantrums or mature insight. Even Raith himself didn't know which one would emerge from the bedclothes. But whichever one it was, the other three dealt with it tolerantly because, in their different ways, they cared about him deeply. Ross would be encouraging and diplomatic, channelling Raith's fears or aggression into work. Mike would often tease. Good-naturedly, he'd wind Raith up, but always watchful, never with malice. Eventually, Raith would see what Mike was doing, and he'd laugh at his own folly.

Phil's MO was different; in ways that none of them quite understood, he was able to calm Raith by sitting with him quietly. He didn't do much, or even say much, and perhaps that was the trick. He offered Raith a peaceful, tranquil space. Raith flowed into it and left his turbulent feelings outside.

It was getting late, and Seabrooke felt he ought to head to his lodgings.

"Do you have to padlock yourself to the case the painting's in?" asked Raith.

"No, but I'll sleep with it under the pillow," he said seriously, and left.

"Was he joking?"

"I think so," said Ross. "We'd better get off, too."

"Are you coming in with us tonight?" Raith asked.

"No."

"But it isn't nice sleeping on your own."

"I'll be fine, and anyway, I'll probably have to get up for Mike a couple of times. I'd only disturb you."

"Ah, that's true," said Raith, backtracking. He hadn't thought about the disruption to his own sleep.

Phil and Ross, knowing exactly how Raith's mind worked, smiled.

"We'll take turns," Phil said firmly, and before Raith could argue, he hugged Ross goodnight and went upstairs.

* * *

By early morning, Ross had been in to see Mike twice. Phil had been in once. Raith had somehow managed to sleep more soundly than he normally did. Phil woke at six a.m. to the sound of further coughing and louder than usual snoring.

"It's not bloody worth it," he said to the room and got up for the second time.

Later, Phil and Ross drove over the back fields to collect the scope and other pieces of equipment. Raith was left to tend to Mike, which he did by sitting as closely to the bedroom door as possible after he'd handed Mike a glass of Lucozade.

"He's not gay," Raith said as Mike, looking a little better, sipped from the glass.

"Who?"

"Nick Seabrooke."

"How do you work that out? Did he say so as in, 'I know you're all gay, but make a move on me and I'll have the lot of you in handcuffs.'?"

"No. I just didn't get a reaction."

"Pardon?"

"He didn't react to me."

"Aye. I got the words. I just wondered what they meant."

"Gay men, or bi men, usually react to me."

"Just because he wasn't foamin' at the mouth doesn't mean he isn't gay."

"I know, but there's usually some reaction. I seem to turn men on."

"Really? You don't turn Ross on. Not sexually."

"Ross is different."

"Ross is gay."

"But Ross never sees past you." It was true—Ross was still as besotted with Mike as he had been the day he met him. "So he's not a good example."

"So, you think that this gay face-recognition technology that some shite governments are thinkin' of usin' to suss out gays is a waste of time, do you? Just stick the poor guy in a room with you and see if his knob goes hard?"

"Well, sort of. I do usually get a reaction."

"Aye. It's probably terror. 'Get this weirdo away from me as fast as possible'."

Raith looked hurt.

"Okay, I know what you mean. You are... you're very charismatic, and people do react to you. You're right, but I think you're makin' a big jump, and what does it matter anyway? He's obviously not bothered by workin' alongside us, and it shouldn't bother you what *he* is."

"It doesn't bother me. I'm just... making an observation, that's all."

* * *

Nick Seabrooke *had* reacted to Raith, to all four men in fact, but Raith was correct: it wasn't his prick that was stimulated. He could appreciate Raith's beauty. Physically, Raith was striking. He was so perfectly proportioned that he looked slightly shorter than his six foot three. Fine features, good hair, he was a stunner all right... in the way that a thoroughbred stallion is stunning, or the lines of a sleek sports car, or the sound of a fine guitar. You wouldn't want sex with any of them. You wouldn't fall in love with them either.

And Phil—he could appreciate the man's intelligence, his grasp of complex theory, his ability to transfer his knowledge into the practicalities of surgery. Nick had done his checks: Phil was a very clever man, as his academic record showed. First name on several research papers, main guest speaker at symposia in Sydney, Montreal and Tokyo, and yet he chose to be one quarter of this strange little quartet stuck in the wilds of North East England. And he'd married Raith! Someone who didn't seem to have half his brainpower.

Seabrooke berated himself: Raith's mental health was suspect, not his brainpower. "Don't confuse the two," he said aloud.

Phil's fondness of Raith was obvious. An interesting man, Doctor Roberts, but in no way sexy. In no way an object of romance.

And much the same could be said of Ross. He clearly possessed the skills to manage everything and everyone with admirably easy grace, and Nick did admire him, but purely in a professional way—nothing more.

Which left Mike—in a sense, the most attractive. Not aesthetically, like Raith. Not intellectually, like Phil. Not 'professionally', like Ross. But Mike was the only one of the four that Nick felt he'd like to get to know better. Perhaps it was because the man was an enigma.

He hadn't noticed the prosthetics at first. They were good. No doubt Phil had had some input there. Nick had only realised when Mike had gathered up the coffee mugs, a little clumsily. Then, surreptitiously, he'd looked more closely. Three right-hand fingers were false. Seabrooke had referred to the violence that Mike had suffered the time he'd brought the photographs. Two years previously—a very nasty business indeed, but not the reason why Detective Inspector Michael Angells had left the Force. The nasty business had happened shortly after.

Seabrooke had been curious. He'd delved into the records and tried to find out more. Why had Mike left? The reason wasn't clear. There were no black marks against his name, and Superintendent Flaxby seemed to be a fan. Mike didn't fall short on the bravery front, that was for sure. An out of the closet, gay, polyamorous cop with, as Ross had told him the first day they'd met, the same tattoo that the other three wore. Ross had said that it was an infinity heart, a visible symbol of their relationship. Their love and passion in the heart. Their honesty and openness in the lemniscate.

A loving relationship and passion—things that, Nick mused, had passed him by. He'd never experienced the joys and pains of either.

He climbed into bed and wondered what they felt like.

* * *

The following morning brought some changes. For a start, Mike was feeling much better. He was up, though looking pale, when Nick knocked on Cromarty's door with the painting.

The sergeant was there in his supervisory and investigative capacity, but it was soon obvious that, with Ross and Phil combining their knowledge, his presence was superfluous.

"If you two ever get bored with your own jobs, you'd be welcome on the fraud squad," he said.

"No thanks. We've seen what being in the police force does to people," Ross quipped, grinning at Mike, who simply said, "Aye."

"I'll go and stretch my legs then," Nick said, and decided to have a little look round Tunhead.

"Raith, why don't you give Nick the tour?" Ross suggested.

Raith thought about this for a moment, then said, "Okay, if he wants."

And, as 'he' did, Raith led the way.

Raith briefly showed Nick his studio, complaining bitterly about the mess the cops had made when they'd 'stolen' his belongings two weeks earlier. Then he knocked at all twelve front doors in the hamlet to show the sergeant what lay behind them. Raith was clearly popular; everyone was concerned about his welfare. Raith almost glowed at their interest. He thrived on being the centre of attention. That much was obvious, but equally obvious was the effect that he had on the BOTWACers. He was dragged inside and hugged. He was plied with cakes and kisses, and those who weren't quite so free with their offerings nevertheless stopped work to ask about his health and safety. Nick felt invisible. Without trying, Raith overshadowed everyone in every room he stood in.

It amused the sergeant that he seemed to be the only person in Tunhead who *didn't* want a piece of Raith! At the top of the Street, he followed Raith along the path to the little church.

"This is where Phil and I got married," Raith stated. "Actually, it isn't. The C of E wouldn't let us get married here. Bigoted lot—half their priests are gay. So we had the ceremony in Tunhope. Then we came here anyway and stuck two fingers up at them."

Nick had noticed the photos in the living room. "There must have been a lot of people packed inside," he remarked, mindful of Raith's popularity.

"No. Well, afterwards, at the party, yes, but at Tunhope and then back here at St Steven's, no. Phil didn't want a lot of people."

Phil didn't want a lot of people. Raith wasn't the alpha male, even though he acted as if he ought to be. "Didn't you mind?"

"No. It was nice the way it was. Do you want to see inside? It's always open."

They had a little look inside the simply furnished building, left by a side entrance and began to wander around the churchyard.

"Someone keeps this tidy," the sergeant remarked, then recalled an item on the rota pinned up in the kitchen.

"We do it," said Raith. "Just the four of us." He paused, not sure if he should continue. "For Khaled and Sam, but..." Another pause "...don't ask Mike about Sam. It'll sound daft, and it isn't. It's just Mike being... loyal."

Another puzzle to add to the ones the sergeant had collected already.

"Khaled and Sam?"

"They're buried here. Do you want to see the quarry?"

A sharp change of subject. Curiosity made Nick wanted to probe. As a guest of the quad, he felt he shouldn't. "If you feel you can go there," he said, diplomatically.

"Today I can go there, yes. Tomorrow might be different."

An interesting piece of self-awareness.

"Yes, I'd like to see it."

The two men walked along the track to the quarry. The quarry was larger than Nick had expected.

"Those early Tunheaders must have been tough as nails," he commented.

"Yeah. Early on it was all worked by hand," Raith explained. "But then they got machinery. Lots of old bits are at the bottom."

"Isn't that dangerous? I mean, for the visitors. Can't you get it cleared?"

"Ross has been trying for years and nobody wants ownership. It's not our property, and we can't touch it. We own the houses, and the land they're built on, and the Street is ours too, to maintain and stuff, but we don't own the church or anything else."

"When you say 'we', you mean the four of you."

This was a statement rather than a question, for, of course, Nick already knew the answer.

"Yes. Everything's joint. Anyway, it's just as well it's full of rubbish, cos I used some on that shite who had the gun." As Raith had said, today he could talk about the incident with equanimity. "Mike's dad was a quarryman. Did you know that?"

Nick did know, but he pretended he didn't to encourage Raith to talk.

"It wasn't here, though. This one was grubbed out long before his dad was quarrying. He worked further along the six-eight-nine. One time, there were lots of quarries. Now, there's just the one big one nearer Warbridge."

"I passed it on the way here," Nick commented. "Hard work."

"Mm. The church is called St Steven's because of the quarry. He was the patron saint of stonemasons. Ross said so. Look!" Raith pointed. "You can see where Mike shot down the slope."

Mike hadn't used one of the gentler tracks, made by sheep and inquisitive people. He'd raced down almost vertically.

"No wonder he came off his bike," said Nick.

"Oh no," said Raith dismissively. "He meant to

come off. He sent the bike one way and rolled the other. Took two of them out at once."

An everyday occurrence, obviously! Nick was impressed.

"You realised who it was?"

"Yes—I customised his helmet. The only other one like that belongs to Ross, and you wouldn't get Ross riding that speed along the level, let alone down that hillside. I didn't realise straight away, but I realised in time to see what he was up to."

Raith sat down on grass that was still damp and relived the scene with actions for the sergeant's benefit.

"It was brave," said Nick.

"No. Just nutty. Mike's as nutty as I am but in a different way," said Raith with a disarming smile.

More self-awareness, and a perfect set of teeth, thought Nick. *I bet they're natural, not cosmetic, too.* Raith was a stunner all right, and Mike was certainly perplexing.

"I think that's it," said Raith.

"It?"

"Tunhead, and my bum's wet."

"Well, thanks for showing me around. It was interesting." Nick began to retrace his steps.

"Oh. No. We can go this way," Raith said, and picking up his bag of BOTWAC cakes, he carried on walking around the rim of the quarry. They joined a track that ran beside the beck and, five minutes later, were climbing over a fence into Cromarty's back garden.

Another little insight into poly-living Tunhead style occurred when they went inside the house.

Raith strode across the kitchen floor, leaving muddy footprints. Mike was standing by the fridge. He said nothing, but reached inside a tall cupboard, extracted a mop and gave Raith the kind of look he might have given criminals.

"It's not my turn," grumbled Raith.

"It's your turn if you can't be arsed to take off your shoes or wipe your feet," said Mike firmly. "Do it."

Raith did it and stalked into the living room to see what Phil and Ross were doing. Nick was still standing at the door. He kicked his shoes off.

"My socks are as clean as a whistle. Shall I come in?" he asked, smiling.

"Aye, of course." Mike returned the smile. "Sorry about that, but he's too big for the naughty step. We have to be very firm with him. He has a tendency to write his own rules."

"You have a lot of rules then?"

"We do. We have to." Mike put the kettle on and explained while he was making a pot of tea. "We don't want this to be just sumwhere where we lay our heads. It's our home, not our house, if that makes sense. Everythin' happens here. Inside Cromarty. We laugh, we argue... we drink gallons of tea... all the normal things that happen when you live with sumbody. I'll be honest, we cry too, and it strikes us that there are so many big things that can give a relationship a bumpy ride that it makes no sense to waste your energy fightin' over the little ones: Who should do the hooverin'? Who should hang the washin' on the line? Who should keep the floor clean? So we have rules. Raith does more than his fair share of grumblin' about it, but it saves a helluva lot of hassle in the long run, believe me."

"So Raith... what? Feels his fame and fortune sets him apart from the daily grind, does he?"

"God no. If he ever tried to play the 'I'm a celebrity' here, I'd crack one of his sculptures over his head! He doesn't think he's above the rules. He just thinks they're irrelevant."

"So, what would you have done if he'd told you to stick your mop up your backside?"

"It sumtimes happens. We ignore him, which he hates, and he'll either do whatever it is himself—with a lot of huffin' and puffin', mind—or if it's sumthin' that can't be put on one side and we've had to do it, eventually he says he's sorry."

"I imagine he says 'sorry' a lot, then."

"No… Raith's… Raith's a great guy. He just doesn't always think. Or rather, he's already thinkin' about the next thing. He's moved on. You're still tryin' to load the washin' machine, he's throwin' the next lot of dirty clothin' into the wash basket. You either accept it or you get wound up about it. We accept it, mostly! I suppose it's one of the benefits of livin' poly. If it was only you and Raith, you'd end up tearin' your hair out. Or his. We just ignore him and talk to sumbody else." Mike poured the tea. "I'll just take these through. Comin'?"

But that evening, Mike did lose his temper with Raith.

"Well, how did your experiment go?" Mike asked, when the sergeant was back in his lodgings.

"My experiment?"

"Well, that's why you gave him the tour, isn't it?"

"I only wanted to know what he is. I wasn't trying to fuck him between the gravestones," Raith said defensively.

"You were trying to find out if he's gay or not?" Ross queried. "That's why you agreed to show him round so readily?"

"No. I know he's not gay. I wanted to know what he is."

Ross and Phil exchanged looks.

"What business is that of yours?" asked Phil.

"It's not my business," Raith admitted, "but I was curious."

"No you weren't," said Mike. "You were just miffed because you couldn't turn him on."

Ross tutted—it was the more likely explanation. "And what did you discover?" he asked.

"See! You're interested too."

"No. I'm just wondering how taking someone round Tunhead can tell you about their orientation."

"Well, I knew he wasn't gay, but I'd say he didn't show any interest in the women either, and he's not on the phone home all the time."

"He's up here on police business. He's not havin' a holiday."

"Yes, but I think he lives on his own. Your old super said he's single, didn't he? I don't think he's with anybody."

"Leave it out, Raith," said Mike.

"But—"

"No. I'm serious. It's none of our business what fuckin' orientation the man is, and we shouldn't even be givin' it the time of day. If you can't fill your mind with sumthin' more useful than wonderin' if a guy is queer, then you're fuckin' pathetic. So quit now. You hear me? Leave. It. Off."

Even Phil looked a bit surprised, and he agreed with Mike.

"But it makes a difference—"

"No. It makes no difference whatsoever. I'm just stunned that you think it does. I'm goin' to bed."

They heard Mike go into the spare bedroom.

"Oops," said Raith. "I didn't mean to get him angry like that."

"No, love," said Phil. "We know. Come here.

He could have put it differently, but he's right."

"No, he's not," Raith said stubbornly. "He's wrong. Saying *what* you are is a part of saying *who* you are. Otherwise, you're pretending to people, and faking causes trouble. Like the painting. You shouldn't fake. So he is wrong. For once."

"That's absolutely true, too," Ross agreed. "You're right, but he was talking about whether it was *our* business or not. Don't forget that when Mike was in CID, he had to deal with a line manager who was the most homophobic cop in the station. Ron Fortune would have made trouble for Mike if Flaxby hadn't been so supportive. It's different for you and me. People in our world are more... tolerant, less reactionary... you know what I mean. And I think we have to be a little extra-sensitive with Mike at the moment. I don't think it's very easy for him to take a backseat in this investigation, especially when the guy in charge would have been under him. Nick is a sergeant. Mike was an inspector."

"And he isn't well," added Phil.

Raith nodded. "Do you think he'd like a cup of cocoa?" he asked, penitent.

"That's a good idea," Phil said. "Why don't you take him one?"

When Raith was safely out of hearing, Ross said, "Mike does not take kindly to being useless."

"You call racing down a quarry being useless?"

"No. But he likes to run things, doesn't he, and I think he's feeling very low."

"That's partly because he's ill, Ross, though he seemed a lot better as the day wore on. You're right, though. Let's hope he appreciates the thought behind the cocoa."

* * *

Raith tapped on the bedroom door. He went in and sat on the edge of the bed.

"Are you asleep?" he whispered.

Mike emerged from the covers and sat up.

"I brought you some cocoa."

"Thank you. I shouldn't 'ave shouted at you," Mike said apologetically.

"No. You were right. It's none of my business what he is."

Mike sighed and took the mug. "Thanks."

Raith tried to explain. "It's just that... Phil and Ross are busy doing stuff. You're kind of out of it, being ill. I've got things to do in the studio, but each time I start, I can't get anywhere. It's like I'm paralysed. Does that make sense?"

"Aye, luv."

"So, I suppose I'm thinking things I shouldn't. Just to use up the time, so I'm not thinking about all this. You know?"

"Aye. I should've thought of that before I shouted at you. You've had a lousy couple of weeks."

"I am pretty pathetic at times, though, aren't I? Fucking stupid."

"No, luv. Bad choice of words. On my part earlier. On your part now. I think you're amazin' actually."

"No!" Raith stretched the word out in disbelief.

"Aye. In all sorts of ways. Not just because you're so creative. I mean, I'd make a mess of drawin' a stick man! But because... you got yourself together and you're really successful. You... you've carved out, literally carved out, this fantastic career. Then there's us. You're one quarter of this fantastic thing that we've got goin' on here. We wouldn't be us without you. Your part in it's crucial. I'm so fuckin' lucky, Raith—lovin', bein' loved. I haven't got much of a job anymore, but I've got Ross and Phil and you, and I know you all love me, and I know you all love each other. I'm sorry I shouted at you, cos I don't know what I'd do without you and that's the truth. You're wonderful. You're not pathetic, and you're not stupid. You're treasured. Really, really treasured, and I'm so sorry I upset you."

The following day, Raith had no trouble being busy in his studio. He never intended to show anyone the painting he completed. Mike's beautiful grey-green eyes, sparkling more than usual, with tears not laughter.

* * *

At two a.m., Ross felt the bed covers move.

"I'll lie on me right. I won't breathe on you," Mike promised.

Ross turned onto his right side too and pressed his body against the warm shape that now lay beside him. He murmured, "Sleep tight," and returned to his dreams.

At three a.m., his mobile rang.

"Bloody hell," said Mike. "If that's what sleepin' with you is like, I'm goin' back to the spare room."

Ross sat up. "I don't recognise the number," he said. "It's probably a wrong one."

"Hit 'later' then."

"No. I'm awake now. Hello?" he said, and listened. "Mike! Mike! Wake up. Listen!"

Chapter 11

Over Weetabix and boiled eggs, Ross told Phil about his nighttime phone call. Raith, it seemed, was up already and working in his studio.

"So this Templeton guy had no idea what's been going on?"

"No! He's been trekking over the Himalayas for the last two months. He didn't even know there was a question mark over the painting, let alone know about Raith."

"Do you believe him? About the painting?"

"It's hard to say. I think so. He was very apologetic about phoning at three in the morning—it was eight a.m. where he is—but he said he felt he'd better contact me as soon as possible."

"And you don't know him personally?"

"No. As I said, he knows one of the people in Brighton that I contacted. He's got a few days in Kathmandu and he was catching up with texts. This was mentioned. He said he realised straight away. He placed the painting with Lenfitte's on the basis of what the client told him about the provenance. She seemed genuine, and her story was perfectly reasonable. He dealt with Lenfitte's by phone and letter, not email. Then, he says, knowing that his lease was coming up, he passed on all his paperwork on to a friend for safe keeping and hit the mountain trail. He doesn't know if the friend collected mail and didn't open it, or if it's just lying on the old shop floor, or if it's been thrown away by new tenants, or what. That, presumably, is why Seabrooke's lot didn't get onto it."

"Communication breakdown."

"Big time."

"We'd better tell him. He'll be over soon."

"Mmm," Mike said.

"I know that 'Mmm'. What's the problem?" asked Ross.

"I don't think we should tell him. Not yet, anyway."

Ross asked, "What?"

Phil asked, "Why?"

"Cos what's he goin' to do? He has to stay with the paintin', so that means the two left in London go and ask the questions."

"Ask Templeton's friend, you mean?"

"Yes, but then ask the woman. They're so fuckin' slow about everythin', this Templeton will have climbed Everest twice before they get their act together. I'd have been bangin' on Lenfitte's doors demandin' to see everythin' connected with the case, secret or not, and I'd have chased up any letters. But also, what if the cop who got suspended isn't the bent one? Nuthin's proved yet. What if it's one of the other two? Then he tells his nasty friends, and this woman's in a lot of trouble. She might have acted in good faith. Even if she hasn't, it's one thing payin' the penalty through the courts. It's another lettin' those animals loose on her."

"Well, if one of Seabrooke's remaining crew's corrupt, Mike, Raith's still in danger. They'll know about the back way into Tunhead over Askill's land."

"No. It was need-to-know only, and as long

as Seabrooke is on the level, which I think he is, they won't know."

"So, what exactly are you saying?"

"Exactly what you think I'm sayin'. We go down south ourselves."

"And how are we going to manage that?" asked Phil. "Seabrooke can't go: he's got to stay with the painting. I can't go: I'm responsible for the Durham equipment, and anyway, I really need to stay with Raith. He can't go, obviously. You can't go: you're not well enough to drive six hundred miles, and that leaves Ross, and I just can't see Ross in the Grand Inquisitor role."

"I'll be all right," said Mike. "I can drive it."

"No, you can't! I'm serious, Mike. You can't be in bed with a temperature one day and drive the length and breadth of England the next. Even if you arrived safely, you'd be too tired to think straight."

"Phil's right, Mike. Look, I've got to go into the gallery for an hour or two this morning, just to make sure things are okay there, but then we could travel down together and share the driving. Stay somewhere overnight and get onto this first thing tomorrow, or even this evening, if we're lucky. I can text Templeton en route and ask him to make sure his friend expects us."

"I suppose so."

"It's a good idea," said Phil.

"Okay, we'll go. Ross and I."

"What do I tell Seabrooke? He'll be over soon."

"Keep quiet as long as you can, but if you have to, say we might have a lead but in case it's a wild goose chase, we didn't want to say anythin', and we knew he couldn't leave, et cetera. In a way that's true, so you won't have to lie."

"Okay. I take it you haven't got any IAM runs. They're not likely to phone you?"

"No. They know I can't do the bikes 'til I sort new transport out. I'll call them when we're travellin' and say I'm still too sick to do the cars. I didn't have anythin' lined up anyway. It would have just been coverin' for others. Let's try and get off before Seabrooke comes over."

As Mike prepared to leave, he said, "Clear away the breakfast dishes, Phil. No time to do it. Seabrooke's got cops' eyes. He'll think we're still in bed."

"Good thinking," said Phil, and did as requested.

* * *

Cromarty's living room was the place to be when wind and rain was lashing down outside, but the kitchen was by far the best location if plenty of light was wanted. Phil had only just managed to fill the dishwasher and set up the FTIR when the sergeant knocked with the painting.

It was late morning before he started to get suspicious.

"Mike feeling bad again?" he asked. "Have Ross and Raith caught it?"

"Raith's been in his studio since daybreak," Phil replied truthfully. "The other two are out."

"Out?"

"They went to the gallery in Gateshead."

"When will they get back?"

"I'm not sure," Phil said evasively.

Seabrooke registered the tone. He withdrew his warrant card from his pocket and—with greater drama than was necessary, Phil thought—placed it on the table.

"Phil," he said gravely, "this is a police investigation. If any of you have information which is relevant to the investigation, you have a duty to tell me. Surely you all know that." He stopped speaking, watched and waited.

"This is the Mike Angells style of questioning, isn't it?" said Phil. "The suspect spills all to escape the unpleasant silence."

"No. It's the Nick Seabrooke style, but it amounts to the same thing. Phil, listen. You four do everything in concert. If Mike and Ross are acting independently of the police, then all four of you will cop it."

He was wrong, but it was the right approach. Phil rushed to Raith's defence.

"No," he said, "we have our little secrets, and we don't always act together, but we do always act on behalf of each other, which is different. Raith knows nothing about this. He was up and out before I got up. I told you the truth about Mike and Ross, too. They went to the gallery, but I don't know what they're doing right this minute. Ross got a phone call. They're following it up, but in case it's a wild goose chase, they went ahead with acting on their own initiative. At the moment, that really is all that I can tell you."

"And, of course, you have no details of this wild goose chase?" Seabrooke asked angrily. Professional anger, and personal too. He didn't deserve to be excluded like this—he'd trusted them. And, of course, he was perfectly right. "For pity's sake, Phil, police are often on wild goose chases. We have to follow every lead, no matter where it takes us! You know it, and I'm sure that Mike bloody Angells knows it."

"He wasn't sure if he could trust you," said Phil quietly. "Not you. The other two. In case the wrong one has been suspended. That's why he didn't tell you. I'm sorry, really."

"I think you'd better tell me everything you know," said the sergeant, somewhat disconcerted by Phil's honesty.

"I basically have done," said Phil. "But, look. I want you to look at something. What do you make of that?"

Seabrooke was looking at a fuchsia-coloured, shield-shaped object that, unmagnified, was thirty-eight microns in width and length.

"There are a few of them," said Phil. "I've sent the spectrum details off to Durham, but they might be a few hours getting back to me. What do you think they are?"

"I think this one might be pollen," said Seabrooke. "Well spotted, Phil. I wonder what they're from."

* * *

Ross and Mike were partway through a long, seven-hour journey.

"That's that settled," said Ross while Mike was taking a turn at the wheel.

"What?"

"We're not going to a hotel. I phoned Melissa. It only seemed right to put her in the picture after she tipped us off and was so helpful the other day. We're spending the night at her house in Sevenoaks. It's only a half hour drive from there to Brighton. Less."

"Okay. What was that you were sayin' about apologisin' though?"

"She's got two bedrooms. She's going to take her daughter's room. We'll have hers, and the daughter's sleeping over at a friend's."

"That is kind of her. Hey, the bedroom won't be pink, will it?"

"And you have the nerve to criticise Raith! Sometimes, Michael Angells, you are so intolerant!"

"No! Never! Me, intolerant?" Mike laughed.

Half an hour later, they were approaching London and the volume of traffic intensified. Mike was a smooth, skilled driver, but his patience and reaction speeds were tested as he dealt with the south easterners' aggressive driving style.

"Did you see that! What the fuck? Shite and bloody onions! Bloody southerners!" Three near misses in quick succession.

Eventually, exclamations had to give way to silent concentration.

"See," said Ross, as they came to a standstill on the approach to the Dartford Bridge, "not just intolerant. Reactionary too. If you're south of the Humber, you want to go home."

"Aye, it's true," Mike admitted. "Down here, I feel out of me comfort zone. It's all too fast and furious for me, and yet, like I said back home, these cops in Seabrooke's crew, they're doin' everythin' so slowly. That side of things, investigations, I'm sure Flaxby would have had us all on it faster. Maybe I'm imaginin' it."

"Maybe you are, yes. I mean, last year, when we were dealing with the trafficking, I remember you saying that the senior officer was dragging his feet. That's why we became involved ourselves."

"True. Traffic crawlin' forward again. That's the Thames is it?" Mike said as they finally crossed the river. "Give me the Wear any day. You're right. I'm a right reactionary northern bugger."

They both laughed and, half an hour later, were parking in front of Melissa Cayson's small front garden.

Her daughter was fifteen and wanted to see

what the visitors looked like before she went to her friend's house for the night. Despite the fact that Pride events were fairly commonplace in her neck of the woods, that gay celebrities were frequently featured in the media, and that these were relatively liberal times, she knew that having two gay men sleeping in her mother's bed would make her an interesting figure at school the following day. Had they been flies on the classroom wall, both Mike and Ross would have been amused and, possibly, bemused as well.

"The one that mum used to work with is really sweet," Melissa's daughter opined to her classmates. "He's not like…" She made mention of various TV personalities whose orientation was suggested visibly in mannerisms and audibly in tone of voice. "I mean, you wouldn't know he was gay. He's got light brown hair, a bit curly, and blue eyes. His name's Ross. The other one is Mike. He hasn't been well, Mum said, and he looked tired. He's tall, big—he'll be the dominant one—and he's got dark brown hair and amazing eyes. I think they're green, but they might not be. I couldn't really stare at him, could I? He didn't say much, being tired, but he's got a real northern accent. He says 'Hellor' instead of 'Hello', and when I asked him if he'd like coffee, he said 'Nor thank you.' He'd 'luv a cup o' tea thor.'"

Mike, who felt as tired as he apparently looked, asked if Melissa would mind if he went up to bed. He fell asleep as soon as his head touched the pillow, and Ross, downstairs, told Melissa what had happened in the past few days.

"So, first thing tomorrow, we'll drive to Brighton to Templeton's friend's house and we'll pick up copies of all the paperwork. Then we'll visit the lady who passed on the painting. She's in

Peacehaven, so it's just a shortish drive along the coast, I think."

"Yes. Not far at all. And she knows you're coming?"

"Yes. Mike was a bit unhappy about that, because if she has got something to hide, she'll have had time to hide it, but we couldn't just turn up on her. We're hardly on a dawn raid."

"No. Of course not. I do hope you can get this all sorted out, Ross."

Just then his mobile rang.

"It's Phil," he said. He listened intently. "Good grief!" he exclaimed. "Well done, you! No, I'll tell him tomorrow. He was knackered. He's gone to bed even though it's only early. Yes, I will. Talk tomorrow. Love you both. Night."

Melissa looked at him inquiringly. "News?"

"Yes, but first, Phil sends best wishes and many thanks to you and your daughter. He saw something on the FTIR. He sent it to Durham. They contacted him an hour ago. It's a microscopic pollen grain. It's from a hornbeam tree. *Carpinus betulus.* He's been checking. Hornbeams don't grow in our part of Durham. It couldn't have fallen onto anything painted locally by Raith, but it could have fallen onto something painted here in southern England."

"Well done Phil! That's really interesting, Ross. It looks as though things are finally moving."

Chapter 12

Nick had intended to eat his meals at Alice's, but he'd remained in Cromarty, like Phil, waiting for some news from Durham. Raith had been pottering round the kitchen for the last hour. His cooking smelt tempting.

"You're welcome to eat here," Phil offered. "Very welcome."

Nick recognised that Phil was apologising for his part in the secrecy. "Thank you," he said. "If you're sure there's enough."

"When Raith's making the meal, we could feed the whole hamlet," Phil assured him. "He measures out in pansful not spoonsful, and we freeze whatever's left. As long as it's not too spicy, that is. Then it goes in the compost bin, though I think it's more likely to kill our plants than aid their growth."

"Very funny," said Raith, "and I've cut the chilli pepper down. If you're staying, can you toss the salad?" he asked Nick.

Phil, meanwhile, spooned pieces of tropical fruit into pretty glass bowls.

"You eat well," the sergeant remarked.

"We try to make the evening meal a proper, sit-down one," Phil explained. "We're not always in together, though and so, sometimes, it's just a sandwich."

The three men sat down, tucked in and chatted.

"That was one of the best meals I've had in ages," said Nick appreciatively when they were all finished.

He had to admit it, he'd enjoyed both the meal and the company. Raith cleared away the uneaten food then went into the living room. Nick wasn't sure if he should follow, or simply say "thank you" and "goodnight." He didn't know if evening cuddles were in order, and he knew he'd find a display of homoerotic affection embarrassing. Phil put three mugs on the worktop, though, so he assumed he was meant to stay.

If cuddles were the norm, they weren't on show that night. Phil sat down next to Raith and placed an arm around his shoulder, but that was the only demonstration of togetherness that occurred. The three men simply talked, and Nick welcomed the opportunity to see this half of the poly quad relaxed and removed from the tensions his presence usually signified.

Again, Nick had to chastise himself for thinking that mentally fragile meant slow-witted. Raith was friendly, amusing, astute and intelligent, even if he was uncomfortably ingenuous.

"You're not gay, are you?" Raith suddenly said. "And I don't think you're straight, either, or bi, and I think you must be ace."

"Sorry," said Phil, embarrassed by Raith's bluntness. "Sometimes Raith says things that most people wouldn't."

"So they think it," Raith said, with a shrug. "What's the difference in thinking it and saying it?"

"Well—" Phil began.

"It's okay, Phil," Nick said. He stared at his coffee mug. He had never discussed being ace with anybody in real life. On internet forums, yes. Often. They'd kept him sane. Real life, no. *Why?*

167

he asked himself. And here was a man who was openly gay—openly polyamorous!—confronting him with his own well-guarded secret. Why couldn't he, like Raith and Phil and Ross and Mike say, *This is me. Like it or leave it. I don't care a toss*?

Here was a chance to say it. *Take it*, he told himself.

"Yes, I'm ace," he said, and immediately wished he hadn't. Of all the people to come out to, he'd chosen two men who surely wouldn't understand at all! Men who knew the taste of other men's saliva and spunk and body sweat, and who doubtless inserted more than fingers and tongues into each other's orifices. Regularly. Not even with just a single other. There were four of them, for goodness sake.

"Oh," said Raith. "I thought you might be. See, I was right," he said to Phil. "I'll go and do the dishes and make some cocoa."

So that was it? That was the big confession? What an anti-climax. Nick could have cried. And they'd obviously been discussing him in his absence!

"I can't imagine it," said Phil gently, aware of Nick's discomfort. "I mean, I fuck the hell out of two sassy men—but if you want to talk about it, I'm a very good listener. I don't reckon it's easy to be asexual in a world that seems to revolve around sex."

"What do you think it revolves around?" asked Nick, relieved, in a way, to turn the conversation from himself.

"For me, it's love, but love, for me, is different from sex. I love Ross. If anything happened to him, I'd be distraught, but I don't find him sexy. The attachment is emotional, deeply emotional, but not sexual."

"I've sometimes felt like that about people," said Nick, drawn into a sort of confession by Phil's quiet, thoughtful manner, "but it hasn't worked out. I've not wanted to... do anything in bed, and they've misunderstood, and we've gone our separate ways. At first, I thought I might be gay, but I know I'm not. I can like men, but not sexually."

"I can like women, but not sexually," Phil said with a laugh.

"Could you kiss one?"

"On the cheek, I could. On the lips—a big sloppy one—ugh! No!"

"Me neither. Ugh! No! The problem is I couldn't do it to a man either."

Phil nodded his understanding.

"There's nothing wrong with my libido," Nick started saying.

"There's nothing *wrong* at all," said Phil.

"Thanks. What I mean is, being ace doesn't mean that I never feel horny. I do. It just means that I'd rather..."

"Slake your own thirst?" Phil finished for him. "That's how Mike would put it anyway."

"Exactly. I've sometimes wondered if the answer would be a QPR. You can have a close attachment, but not a sexual one, and all those other needs would be catered for. The emotional ones, for example."

"Mm. It has attraction. You can form close friendships, be supportive, be supported... Speaking personally, I'd find it difficult. Asking a single other to supply all my needs... it's asking a lot. That's why a poly works so well for me."

"I think I'd find *that* difficult. I'm used to having my own space."

"It's not the biggest issue, not with miles of

moorland on the doorstep. We each have our favourite spots."

"Ross doesn't," said Raith, returning to the room with mugs of cocoa. "He doesn't seem to need own time."

"That's true, actually. I have no experience of a QPR as such, although, in a sense, it's what I have with Ross. You're right, though. Living closely with other people, in a relationship like ours—you have to really want it. It's hard work, I can tell you that! We don't always see eye to eye. We have to compromise a lot, but it's very different from living in a normal family. There's no traditional hierarchy to govern expectations. That is, there's no age-related hierarchy, and no finance-related hierarchy and no gender-related one either. The UK's still pretty male-dommed, even if people prefer to think otherwise."

"There's a fucking Mike-related hierarchy," Raith moaned. "He can be bloody bossy. You'd think we were criminals, the way he lays down the law at times."

"He likes to get things moving. In one sense, he's a doer rather than a thinker," said Phil in Mike's defence.

"He just doesn't understand the creative mind," said Raith, with a toss of his hair.

"That's probably true." Phil gave Raith a squeeze. "The thing is, we're four men and we're ostensibly equal, but it isn't quite as straightforward as that statement makes it seem. There are always going to be the people who were in the relationship first, and the people who come after. To be honest, that caused us—or, rather, me—a hell of a lot of problems last year. We dealt with it though."

"We got married," said Raith, squeezing Phil back.

Nick didn't press for details. Instead, he said, "Your personalities must play a huge part. You say that Mike has strong opinions…" *Why am I focusing on Mike?* he wondered.

"Yes, but he never forces them on us, despite what Raith's just implied. On really important issues, we take a vote, and Mike always abides by the majority decision."

"What if the vote is split down the middle?"

"Then we toss a coin. If one side's arguments are as good as the other side's, what's the point of arguing about them any further? It's worked for us so far."

"Obviously. What did you mean when you said you have to really want it?"

"I suppose I meant that we really want—we need—each other, and we know it. You could say that we're very demanding. In a variety of ways. A relationship with just a single person… it would place a heavy burden on that person's shoulders. For me, it's… well, I grew up feeling guilty, really guilty, about being gay. I married the daughter of friends of my parents partly to please everyone, partly to convince myself that I was normal. The whole thing was disastrous and just reinforced my negative feelings. Then these three came along. First Mike, then Ross and Raith, and they were all so easy with their sexuality. I don't mean that they went around waving Gay Pride banners in people's faces."

"I've done that," said Raith. "So has Ross."

"I hope not! He means they've been on marches, Nick. What I mean is: they never tried to hide it. Not even Mike, and he was a cop with a homophobic boss. I was so envious! It just gradually washed off on me, and each of them played a part in helping me to throw away the baggage. I think that getting married to Raith, standing up and saying 'I do' to another man, going on our honeymoon and checking in as a couple... I can't tell you how doing those things made me feel." He didn't need to tell. It was obvious. "We were going to go to Venezuela for our anniversary, and in a way, it's probably a good thing that we didn't. I'd probably have had an argument with immigration because we wouldn't have been able to enter the country as a married couple. I can stand up for gay rights now. I'd have hidden in a corner not so long ago."

Like I do, thought Nick.

"Phil and Ross and Mike all help me," said Raith. "I'd be hard work for just one person, wouldn't I, Phil?"

"Just a bit."

Raith clearly felt that the reasons were self-evident. He moved on to Ross. "Ross thought he only needed Mike. He's always been fond of me, but I don't think he ever thought he needed me, or needed Phil, but things happened a couple of years ago that really shook him up, didn't they, Phil?"

"Yes."

Nick caught the warning look. He assumed that the 'things' referred to more than Mike's resignation from the police force and his treatment at Raith's ex-lover's hands. Again, he didn't press. Instead, he said, "And Mike himself?"

"Oh, Mike's the neediest of all of us," said Raith enigmatically and collected up the cocoa mugs. Nick was puzzled and he wanted to know more, but he felt he'd been given a hint to go. He took it.

"Thank you again for a great meal," he said at the door.

"Phil's cooking tomorrow," said Raith, "so I

think it'll be fish. He says it's better than vegi. If that's okay, you're very welcome."

"If you're sure you don't mind..."

"Don't mind at all," said Raith, with a friendly smile. "Night night."

"Goodnight."

Nick began to walk uphill. The Street was almost in darkness. Cromarty's thick curtains shut out most of the light from the living room, and Tunhead's other residents clearly liked to shut the night out too. Nick glanced back down the lane as a beam of light from the bedroom window lit up the cobblestones. Then even the bedroom curtains were drawn, and the village street returned to darkness. Nick knocked lightly on Alice's door and waited to be let in.

Back in Cromarty, Phil affectionately wagged a finger at Raith. "Listen, you," he said. "When Ross and Mike get back, no discussing Nick's sexuality in front of them."

"Don't you mean his asexuality?"

"You know exactly what I mean. I don't think he's ready to have his sex life discussed by four men he only met two weeks ago."

"His lack of sex life."

"Raith!"

"Okay. Okay. I hear what you're saying. Why is he so bothered, though? It's not like being gay, is it? I mean, you don't get beaten up for being asexual, or forced to undergo conversion therapy, or get whipped in public, or thrown into jail. And it fucking hurts, getting fucked. Well, it does at first anyway. It's not the same thing, is it? And it's never been illegal. So why all the fuss and secrecy?"

If Raith had only known it, the sergeant was trying to answer that very question himself.

He'd had to deal with people's ignorance and prejudice too. He'd tried to talk about asexuality with some people, in a non-committal, third-person sort of way, but their responses made him wish he hadn't bothered. They told him that aces hadn't met the right person yet, or that they were too fussy and never satisfied. They told him that aces were prudish or needed to buy some Viagra. Two had assumed that some childhood trauma must be at the heart of what they saw as asexuals' 'problems'. Occasionally, they'd become suspicious and started asking personal questions: Why his interest? Why didn't he date as much as they did? He'd made excuses—pressure of work, lack of leisure time, et cetera. At least it shut people up.

He wasn't overly fussy. He knew he wasn't prudish. He hadn't, thank God, been subjected to anything that might have made him sex repulsed. He could see that he was averse to indulging in some aspects of 'the requirements', but from what Phil had said, laughing, he was too. But Phil had Raith, and Ross and Mike. Nick, instead, had no one.

He thought about what Phil had said about the quad's importance. Nick didn't need three more people. He'd never really thought he needed *one*, but perhaps he did. Another person at his side. Someone who would stand up with a hand on his shoulder and say, *"I'm ace too, and you can stick your stupid ignorance where it hurts!"*

But where would he find that other person? He was a cop; he had to be circumspect in his dealings with others.

"You need other people to support you, Nick," he told himself. "That's the bottom line. Some folk manage to deal with their orientation themselves—the Mikes and Rosses and Raiths of this world—but perhaps you're more like Phil and you need a little outside help."

It wasn't just Phil who had needed help, though. What had Raith said about Mike? He'd called Mike the neediest of all of them. He wondered what Raith had meant by that.

Still speculating, he fell asleep.

Chapter 13

Early on Sunday morning, Ross and Mike drove to Brighton and collected everything of relevance that had been left with Templeton's friend. Then they drove to Peacehaven. As Templeton had promised, he'd contacted the seller, a Mrs Susan Osgood, to advise her of their visit. She opened her door to two immaculately dressed men.

"Mrs Osgood?" said the smaller one. "I'm Ross Whitburn-Howe, the gallery owner who is looking after Mr Templeton's affairs until he returns from the Far East, and this is my associate, Michael Angells."

Mike smiled, in part at the description, and said, "Good mornin'."

Ross apologised for disturbing her on a Sunday. It wasn't a problem, she said, and ushered them into the lounge where another woman was waiting.

"This is my niece, Sally," she said. "I'm a little uncertain about business matters, so…"

"Absolutely," said Ross, thinking, *How uncertain, I wonder?*

The niece, like the two men, was in her thirties. She greeted them with a smile, a handshake, and an offer of tea, which Mike, still dry-throated from his bout of 'man flu', gratefully accepted.

Ross declined and asked for a glass of water. "Tap is fine."

He hadn't prepared a spiel. His conversation

flowed naturally as, of course, it ought to have done: he was simply doing his normal job. He explained that, for purposes of cataloguing, the painting's provenance needed to be clarified, and he needed as much detail as possible.

"I understand that you found the Ivashova when you were throwing out some boxes from the loft," he said encouragingly, and waited.

Mrs Osgood had found the painting in a large tin box, along with her father's army things. She had the box, and showed Ross and Mike the remaining contents, and told them a little of her father's history.

Mike was curious about the flash—the fabric badge that army personnel wore on their uniform. It was a stylised union flag on a black background with, in silver, the word BRIXMIS.

"What's BRIXMIS?" he asked. "It sounds like Brexit."

"No! It was about working together, not working separately," Mrs Osgood explained. "Dad was part of a liaison unit that operated behind the Iron Curtain in East Germany during the Cold War. I had to look the name up myself. It was the British Commanders'-in-Chief Mission to the Soviet Forces in Germany. Dad wasn't a commander. He was just a regular, uniformed soldier, and he was one of the drivers." She went on to explain that she thought her father had got the painting because of his role in the unit. "Dad used to say that most of the liaison work took place at formal events like parades and official parties, but also, sometimes, there were 'cultural tours' and the bigwigs would stay in hotels in some of the larger East German cities. He'd go too, as the driver, and he got to know members of the Soviet armed forces and some of the civilians. I think that perhaps one of them gave him the painting. I don't know why."

"It's more than possible," said Ross thoughtfully, ostensibly agreeing with the explanation. "A lot of Soviet painters had their output destroyed during Stalin's time, and people may have tried to smuggle work out of the country."

"That's what I wondered, too," said Mrs Osgood.

"So, there was no paperwork to accompany the painting?" Ross asked, apparently investigating the contents of the tin box.

"No, nothing."

"And you took the painting to Templeton's Fine Arts…?"

"Well, I'd never heard of this Ivashova lady, but I was curious and I looked her up. When I saw that she was Russian, I thought it might be worth seeing if it was valuable."

Ross nodded.

"He—Mr Templeton—said that there was a particular London auctioneers who were interested in Russian painters, and I said 'send it to them, then'."

"Was there a reason why you asked for the transaction to be private?"

"Well, I thought, if it is valuable, I don't want reporters and people knocking at my door. Then Mr Templeton contacted me to say that he'd given the painting to the auctioneers, and he would contact me again on return from his holiday."

"Yes," said Ross. "I have a copy of his letter here. Can you tell us anything else about the painting?"

"No, not really. That's all I know."

There was a lull, broken by the niece.

"Aunty Sue is a good painter, herself. Aren't you, Aunty?"

"No! I just dabble," said Mrs Osgood modestly.

"Are these yours?" Ross asked, referring to the dozen or so paintings that brightened the walls of the lounge. 'Brightened' was the operative word, as both the men had realised as soon as they'd walked in the room: the paintings were unusually colourful.

"Most of them are. Two or three of them are Dad's."

"You father was an artist, too?"

"He wouldn't have called himself one. He enjoyed painting though, even when he was old. There was nothing wrong with his eyes or his hands, but his legs were bad. I used to take him to the local woods, and I'd leave him there for an hour or so while I walked the dog."

"May we look?"

Ross studied each of the paintings in turn. Mike stood at his side, pretending to be knowledgeable as Ross made comments about perspective and composition, but not about colour.

"These three are your father's, I presume," said Ross, pointing to a group of paintings of trees.

"Yes. It's a local Woodland Trust site. It's pretty."

"Do you sell your works?" Ross asked.

She didn't.

Ross pointed to three of them. "I'll buy these off you right now," he said. "Nine hundred pounds for the three of them. Three hundred each."

"You'll...! Nine hundred pounds?"

"Aunty," said Mrs Osgood's niece. "If Mr Whitburn-Howe thinks they're good, and he can sell them, sell them!"

Oh, Ross would be able to sell them, all right. And turn a nice, fat profit.

"I'll transfer the money into your bank account right now if you'll let me take them with me."

She was retired... She was unhappy providing

personal information... She was very apologetic, but she was reluctant to give details of her bank account...

"Very wise," said Mike gravely.

"Understandable," said Ross, "though I use an app."

"Transfer it to my account," Sally offered.

The deal was done and soon, after thanking Mrs Osgood and her niece for their time, the two men left.

"There were some really old paints in that tin box," said Ross when they were seated in the car. "Interesting. Do you reckon we've time for a wander in the woods? I'm just looking up Woodland Trust sites," he added. "Local ones."

"You think there'll be hornbeams there?"

"More than likely. The fruits are pretty, and I wouldn't mind betting they're still on the trees at this time of year round here. They look like those frilly pantaloons that ladies used to wear."

"I wouldn't know," said Mike with mock disdain. "How the hell do *you* know all these things? It doesn't matter what it is, you know sumthin' about it! Just amazes me."

"I don't know, really. I just do. Mind you, I have big gaps in my knowledge." Ross laughed.

"Oh, aye? Such as?"

"Well, we've still got a load of positions to try."

"Naughty as well as knowledgeable. Hm. Incidentally, why did you choose those three paintings?"

"The pollen," Ross answered. "She must have painted the fake Ivashova in the spring when the tree pollen count was high, and two of the ones I bought had bluebells."

"Hey! Well done you! A proper detective. The other one?"

"The seascape? I liked it. It wasn't bad at all. Turn left here. By the way, I could have kicked you when you said that she was wise not providing details of her banking," said Ross as they drove to the woods.

"It's true," said Mike. "We could be anybody."

"Yes, but…"

"For all she knows, we're scammers."

"Like her!"

"Oh, aye, definitely like her!"

* * *

Susan Osgood was a widow of sixty-six. Her husband had died from a heart attack five years earlier. She hadn't any children of her own, but Sally could almost be called one. She'd jollied her aunty out of some of her grief, and—at Sally's suggestion— Aunty Sue had booked an activity holiday with TL Travel, a company that specialised in activity holidays for people like herself. She'd tried walking in Yorkshire, folk dancing in Cornwall and choral singing in Glamorgan, and she had enjoyed the experiences so much that she'd decided to be more adventurous. She'd scrolled through the online brochure and been drawn to "The Art and Architecture of Warsaw and St Petersburg". Seven days away and—as always, with TL Travel—all entry fees and meals and snacks included. She went, and she returned.

She'd been very taken with some paintings hanging in a St Petersburg gallery. *I paint a bit like that*, she thought. She'd bought some postcards from the ground floor shop and, back home in Peacehaven, embarked on a painting of her own in a similar style.

In fact, she'd always painted in that style. Doing so, it seemed, had been her problem. She'd tried to get into art school in her youth, but her applications had always been refused. It seemed to her that, these days, further education was regarded as a right. In her day, it wasn't. Occasional forays into adult education hadn't helped her confidence: tutors encouraged her to tone her colours down. *"You'll never sell your work if you paint like that,"* she was told, and they were right: she couldn't sell her work. She tried. So she painted for her own enjoyment and, after a suitably lengthy curing time, varnished the pictures and hung them on the wall. Hung all except one, that is.

The exception had stayed in her bedroom. She'd had other things on her mind. Her then very elderly father was intending to move in to her bungalow. He needed looking after. Unfortunately, the move never happened, for, aged ninety-three, he died. So Susan continued the task she had already started—clearing out her dad's house to put it up for sale. Finally, in May, the task was done.

In June, Susan had taken another trip. This one was to Templeton's gallery in Brighton, much closer to her South Downs home than St Petersburg and Warsaw had been. Instead of a travel case, she carried a canvas shoulder bag.

She smiled at the assistant, handed him a canvas and hesitantly asked, "Do you think this could be worth anything? I found it in the attic in a box of my old dad's military gear. It reminded me of a painting I saw last year on holiday."

The assistant didn't recognise the name scrawled in the bottom right-hand corner, but he sensed that it was Eastern European, and he knew that rich Russian oligarchs paid good money for long-lost Russian works of art. Just the previous spring, a Chagall had doubled its estimate in Paris.

"Could you leave it with me?" he asked. "I don't know the artist, but I'll do my homework and get back to you. It's an interesting painting!"

Susan Osgood smiled and went home to paint another.

* * *

Mike and Ross were still a good few hours' drive from home as Phil, Raith and Nick finished off what Phil called 'Trawlerman Pie'. Raith and Nick went into the living room while Phil cleared away the dishes.

"Wouldn't it be fairer to split the kitchen duties?" asked the sergeant. "One person cooks, everybody eats, and another person clears away?"

"No," said Raith dismissively. "Everybody doesn't eat, and that's the problem. I'd cook something, but half an hour before it's on the table, Phil phones, or Mike would phone when he was a cop, and say they were delayed. They'd use the microwave when they got back. So then they can't do their turn on the rota, and then there's a fuss and palaver and it's 'I did it yesterday. I'm not doing it two days on the trot,' and it just doesn't work. Ross says our mantra should be 'Minimise dissention', and this is the best way to do it."

"Ah. I see."

"But you should have thought of that. You being a detective," Raith said.

"It's hard to feel like a detective up here," Nick

admitted. There was at least one other question he wanted answering, though. Raith was blunt. Nick would be too. "What did you mean yesterday when you said that Mike was very needy?" he asked.

Raith didn't answer. Indeed, he looked uncomfortable. "Maybe you better ask Phil. He'd explain it better than me."

But Nick had the feeling that Phil would be equally evasive. He'd have to work it out without their help.

As the senior investigating officer, he had every reason to stay at Cromarty, wait for Ross and Mike to return and give them another piece of his mind. The trouble was, one piece of his mind was focused on Mike for a non-professional reason.

He returned to Alice's and was still awake when he heard the rumble of a four by four nearing the hamlet from over the fields. In his role as Raith's guardian, he felt he ought to check that it was Ross and Mike, not someone else who had bypassed the lane and its barrier. He peeped through a gap in the curtains. It was them. He went back to bed.

He tossed. He turned. If he hadn't been in someone else's house at two o'clock in the morning, he'd have been pacing up and down.

You hardly know the ruddy man! he told himself. It was true. He'd been in Mike's company... how long? A couple of hours the day they'd met. Several hours since, but Mike had spent most of Wednesday and Thursday ill in bed, and had been away from Tunhead altogether for most of the last two days. A grand total of... Nick counted the hours up. Eight.

So why was Mike Angells so constantly in his thoughts?

He tried to be rational. The man had been a CID

detective. That held some obvious fascination, and his career had been an interesting one—a steady rise from uniformed constable via Highways Patrol to plain-clothes inspector, without the aid of a uni degree to help him on his way. Awards for bravery, commendations for the tightness of his cases... one referral to the IPCC, as it was, but it hadn't come to anything. All good, but then he'd chucked the badge in two years ago. Why? To work for the IAM at a fraction of the salary? Not likely. And did Nick really want to know the answer? It was none of his business. The problem was, the man was on his mind and he couldn't work out why.

It isn't love! he told himself for the umpteenth time. *I'm ace, though that's no barrier. If past experience is anything to go by, though, I'm not particularly romantic. I don't mind somebody's arm on my shoulders, or around me, but I don't want to snuggle up naked, or be deep kissed by anyone, and certainly not by Mike Angells.*

The thought of Mike's hands on his skin was unpleasant. The thought of Mike's tongue in his mouth was horrendous, and as for sex, that degree and sort of intimacy... If Mike came towards him waggling his prick, he'd turn and walk out the room. Or arrest him for indecent exposure! So, what the hell was it? Another crush? Another squish?

"I'm thirty ruddy four," he said aloud. "I'm not a schoolkid."

Well, he had one or two days left, at most, to explain his infatuation.

The cockerels were crowing by the time he fell asleep.

* * *

If the sergeant expected a sheepish apology when, on Monday morning, he met the two men face to face, he didn't get it. They were defiant. What's more, both Raith and Phil had had time to examine the paintings Ross had bought. Mike listed the evidence, ticking each point off on his fingers: the proximity of hornbeam, the presence of pollen grains, the thread count of the canvas, the nature of the brush strokes and, most important, the fact that the woman, this Susan Osgood, appeared to be tetrachromatic.

"And there's something else," said Ross. "According to Templeton, she told him that the painting resembled some that she'd seen on holiday the previous year. Surely you can find out where she went. If Ivashovas were on display…"

"We know that you'd still need a confession," Mike admitted. "Most of that stuff is circumstantial, but we've met her. We think you'd get one, especially if you told her the harm her actions could have caused to Raith."

"Will she go to jail?" asked Raith.

"It's an indictable offence," Mike replied sternly. "Probably, yes."

"But if she's old, and nice and stuff…"

"She nearly got you killed," said Mike. "There's nothing more to say."

Still thinks like a cop, thought Nick. *A crime. A punishment*.

* * *

As it transpired, Susan Osgood didn't get imprisoned. When she discovered how, because of her intention to deceive, an innocent man had been kidnapped, assaulted and, at one stage, held at gunpoint, she was overcome with guilt and remorse. The defence made much of her reaction, her previous good character, and the fact that her father's recent death might have clouded her judgement. The judge was confident that her actions would never be repeated. To Mrs Osgood's and her niece, Sally's, great relief, the sentence was two years, suspended.

But between the solving of the case at the tail end of October, and the judgement the following May, life in Tunhead continued to be, intermittently, eventful.

Chapter 14

Phil still had a week of his holiday remaining, but he wanted nothing more than a return to peace and quiet. So, having handed the FTIR back to its rightful owner, he spent his time lying in bed, watching TV, lounging around Cromarty and, weather permitting, walking over the moors with whichever of the other men had the time and the inclination to go too.

On one of these walks, when Ross and Raith had driven off to Ross's gallery together, Phil and Mike walked to Harnell Force. Phil's injuries, sustained in that very spot the previous year, still caused him to limp a little. It had been the scene of a tragedy.

"You okay?" asked Mike.

"I'll manage," said Phil. "You might need to carry me home, though."

"I didn't mean your leg."

"Oh." Phil pulled a face. "Yes. I'm okay. It seems ages ago. Time goes so quickly." After a pause, he added, "I do think about it, yes, and I feel sad when I do so, but… you have to move on, don't you?"

Mike looked at him. "Are you tellin' that to yourself, or to me? Given that we've both got our skeletons in the cupboard. In Tunhead graveyard anyway."

"I've moved on," said Phil, "and so have you."

"I still think about him though," said Mike. "Even though I've got you and Raith and Ross, and I love the three of you to bits, I still think about him. Why? Why can't I let it go completely, heh?"

The two men sat down on a bare rock out of the spray of the waterfall.

"I don't really know why, love," Phil admitted. "Because you're you, I suppose."

"Sumtimes I think I'm as nuts as Raith. He's obsessed with chilli flakes. I'm obsessed with a dead lover."

"Are you worried about it? Worried about worrying about it, that is."

"In a way. It's almost like... I'm insultin' you three, not bein' able to give up on it."

"Well, I don't feel insulted, and I'm sure that Ross doesn't, and it wouldn't even occur to Raith to be insulted by anything you did. You know that."

"Aye. Ta."

"But... perhaps being so physically close, close to the grave, seeing the churchyard every day, perhaps that hasn't helped you to get over it, and your old job—I mean, how many road accidents must you have seen? Every single one must have brought Sam's death back."

Sam had been killed by a drunk driver, pinned between a wall and the bonnet of a car in a club car park. Mike had only been gone a minute, bringing his bike around.

"I'll be honest. Every fuckin' time I see a crash, it flashes past me. It's fuckin' stupid, isn't it? It happened years ago."

"Hey, come on. Wipe those tears," Phil said gently.

Mike nodded and did so.

"Oh, I dunno, Phil," he said. "People who see us... They must think... Well, they probably think that I'm big and tough, roarin' round on a bike, havin' been a cop, and that's a joke, cos sumtimes I don't feel tough at all. I'd be a crumblin' wreck if I didn't have you three."

"I think you're tough. I mean, last year with that creep who tried to blackmail me, and the way you've acted the past three weeks… seems pretty tough to me."

"That was desperation, Phil, and you know it! If anyone tries to hurt you, or hurt Raith, or hurt Ross, I'll risk everythin' to stop 'em. I was talkin' about it to Ross—whether I do things just because I'm selfish and don't want to lose our quad. If we broke up, I might as well just be another body in the graveyard."

"I do understand that. You know I do. It doesn't say much for us as individuals, does it? Most people get along fine with the help of a single other or, like Nick Seabrooke, manage to cope on their own—though I'm not totally sure that he's coping on his own. He was very interested in you, by the way."

"Oh aye?"

"He was pumping me a bit."

"Oh? He was okay really, wasn't he? I mean, he was helpful, and he could have really bawled Ross and me out over what we did."

"Mm. He'd vented most of his fury by the time he got to you two, but yes, he was fine." *He'd have been very interested in what you've just been saying,* Phil thought. He checked the time on his brand-new watch.

"It's a great watch, that, Phil. It's beautiful."

"I know. I feel quite emotional just looking at it. I couldn't begin to design something so exquisite. Clever Raith, heh? He and Ross will be back soon, demanding food no doubt." He glanced around him. "Doesn't putting the hour forward make a change? It's already growing dark. We'd better make a move."

The two men stood up.

"It's not exactly the Angel Falls, is it, Phil? I'm sorry it all went wrong."

"There's always next year. At least he's safe. That's the important thing. God, I'm stiff," said Phil, stretching.

"You need to see a doctor. He might be able to give you sumthin'."

"Very funny. You can give me a piggy back if I start to struggle."

"You're jestin'! I doubt if I could give me brother's kids a piggy back the way I feel at the moment. I've still got a bit of that bug."

"Now you're sounding like Raith!"

"No. He'd still have a lot of the bug."

Laughing, and trading jokes, they made their way home.

* * *

The only eventful occurrence the following week was a news item. According to the BBC, Danik Amelin, the prize-winning architect whose most recent designs included the two newest office blocks in Dubai, had been found dead in his London office. A Scotland Yard pathologist stated that the death was due to a heroin overdose. Police thought the drug was self-administered. Mr Amelin had been under investigation with regard to the kidnapping of the ceramicist and artist, Raith Balan, and was reportedly suffering from strain. The national papers carried similar snippets.

Raith said, "Good riddance."

Mike said nothing. The suicide of a man with connections to criminals seemed, to him, suspicious, but he kept his thoughts to himself.

The next eventful occurrence occurred in mid-November—the return of DS Seabrooke.

"I'm here on business," he said on the phone, "and I'd like to come and talk to you."

'I'd like talk to you' had a difference ambience from 'I'd like to see you' and the quad were chary regarding the sergeant's intent. Rightly so.

He took a long time getting to the point. Despite Mike's prompting, he refused to be drawn on the official line over Amelin's death. Instead, he spoke about the fact that the fraud squad dealt increasingly with cybercrime. He talked in general about money laundering and drug and arms cartels. He talked about everything but paintings.

"Will you stop fluffin' about," said Mike, running out of patience. "Tell us why you're here."

"We want Raith to forge an Ivashova," Seabrooke said.

There was a pause.

"I obviously misheard you," Phil said. "You didn't say you wanted to involve Raith in more stupid crap, did you?"

"Not 'stupid crap', no, but you did hear right."

"No," said Phil emphatically. "No."

"No way," said Mike and Ross, almost in unison.

Raith said nothing. He just looked stunned.

The sergeant explained the thinking behind the request. It was an opportunity to get at some of the big people, to get some names, to break up at least one cell... What they needed was a painting.

"But any painting would do," said Ross. "Why use a forged Ivashova? Why involve Raith?"

"Because, right now, and because of this case, that's where the interest is lying. Not with Chagalls or Maleviches, but with these weirdly coloured landscapes that hardly anyone else can produce. They're rare by default. Ask your contacts, Ross. They'll all tell you the same thing. Here's an advance copy of December's *Frameworks* magazine." He extracted it from his briefcase.

"Frameworks? Nice title." Mike observed. "Someone's got a sense of humour."

"The cover page—an Ivashova. Prices are going to shoot through the roof, and the higher they shoot, the more attractive to anyone in the money laundering business."

The cover depicted a snow scene, but snow Ivashova-style had all the hues of nacreous clouds that continue shining after sunset.

"It's in the Tretyakov," said Seabrooke.

"Moscow," said Ross, answering the other men's bemused looks.

There was more uneasy talk and further explanation.

"We need to discuss it," said Mike. "On our own."

"Of course," said the sergeant. "I'm staying in Warbridge. Contact me when you've made a decision, but I absolutely guarantee that Raith's name will be kept completely out of this if you agree to run with it."

It didn't surprise him that he wasn't invited to stay for tea. He said his goodbyes and left.

* * *

"Well," said Raith. "I don't know what to do."

"I'd rather you had nothing to do with it, love,"

Phil stated. "I've nothing else to say."

"We have to talk about it, Phil. Seabrooke wants a decision," said Mike. "Ross?"

"It all depends on how certain we are that Raith would be safe. From what the sergeant said, no one would know that Raith had done the painting except us, his crew and the undercover cop. Everyone else, including the press, would be told that the work was genuine."

"What if the money launderers don't want another deal?" asked Phil. "There's no guarantee that they will."

"Then, accordin' to Seabrooke, the sale would be withdrawn, the Balanova would be destroyed and that's the end of the affair. He was pretty sure they'd bite, though."

"Balanova?"

"Well, that's sort of what it is," said Mike.

"I suppose the three you dealt with in the quarry aren't likely to furnish any information, are they?" said Ross. "That wasn't really a question."

"Well I wouldn't say anythin' if I was them," said Mike. "They'll do their stretch, and when they come out, there'll be a nice fat balance in their bank accounts."

"And they say that crime doesn't pay," said Phil. "You sound as though you're in favour of Raith's involvement, Mike," he added, a little critically.

"No, not at all. Or rather, that wasn't my intention. Havin' said that, I suppose I am comin' at it more from Seabrook's angle. If I was the SIO, I'd be wantin' to explore every single avenue to get hold of money launderin' shiters, so I'm sympathetic, but that doesn't mean I'd be wantin' Raith to do it. Anyway, it isn't up to me. It's up to us."

Phil was persistent. "If they, as you put it, bite, how does it show that they're the money launderers though? They buy a painting. So do thousands of perfectly innocent people."

"Aye, but, at the moment, and especially with Amelin dead, the police have no idea who the shiters are, do they? As Seabrooke says, there'll be an undercover guy. He'll throw Amelin's name around, et cetera. Make a link. The bosses of the three who grabbed Raith are the only ones who are likely to rise to that particular bait. The hope is that they'll make contact."

"So you're saying that Amelin's death actually did the police a favour?"

"I suppose so. Aye. It gives them a name to hang the scam on."

"Seabrooke was very cagey about his death. It makes me think that it wasn't suicide," said Ross. "Do you think he knew more than he was letting on?"

"I don't know," said Mike, "and I'm not willin' to speculate." Not aloud, anyway. He'd done plenty of thinking quietly.

"Do you think the money launderers killed him?" asked Raith. He'd been very quiet.

"I don't know," Mike repeated. "*We* don't know."

"The guy who's undercover is taking a risk if they did have a hand in the death," said Ross.

"Aye, but that's what cops do," said Mike. "Take risks, but only calculated ones. Well? Any more to say?"

Ross, Phil and Raith shook their heads.

"Raith?"

"I'll do it if we're sure that I'll be safe," said Raith. "As long as my name's not involved. There won't be time to varnish a painting though, not with the time scale he wanted."

"Ross?"

"Same as Raith. As long as he's safe and his name's kept right out of it."

"Phil?"

"No."

"Your call, Mike," said Ross.

"I'm with you two. I think Raith will be safe."

Phil stood up and walked out of the room. The three who remained exchanged looks.

"Do you want to phone Seabrooke, Raith?" asked Mike.

"The sergeant?"

"Mm."

"Not really. Will you?"

"Are you still takin' me into Warbridge, tomorrow, Ross, on your way in? I'll go with Phil if it's awkward." Mike had arranged to look at a new bike.

"No, it's fine."

"Then I'll double-check the safeguards and, as long as I'm satisfied, I'll tell him you'll do it—shall I, Raith?"

"As long as it's safe."

Mike sent Seabrooke a text and didn't have to wait for a reply. It came immediately. He read it and put his phone away.

"Sorted. I'll deal with it tomorrow. Raith, swap beds tonight, heh?"

"Phil's upset, isn't he?"

"He's worried about you, that's all. He isn't very fond of the police at the moment."

"No. You and Ross feel I'll be fine, though, don't you?"

"Sure, but I'll double-check, and only if I'm totally, one hundred and ten per cent certain, will I say you'll do it."

"Okay."

So, that night, Raith slept with Ross, and Mike went in to Phil.

"I figured you'd make him nervous," Mike said

as he opened the bedroom door. "And he has to decide without our pressure."

"I'm right to make him nervous. Seabrooke's involvement so far hasn't been exactly brilliant."

Phil was sitting on the bed, fully dressed. His eyes followed Mike's movements as he closed the door and stripped. The room was warm and cosy even though it was November. Mike stretched out at Phil's side.

"Come on," he said gently. "Relax."

"I don't feel relaxed."

"Nuthin' will happen to him."

"Mmm." Phil wasn't convinced. "There are times when you are all cop. You want to catch the bad guys, and I can see that Seabrooke's just the same. I don't want Raith to be a lamb to your slaughter."

"Won't happen. No one will even know, except us and his crew. They've already kicked the bad apple out of there—the one who knew Charles King."

"Yes, I know, but… "

"Come here. Do what you want. Whatever'll make you feel better."

"It's not the answer to everything, you know."

"No? Solves most of *my* problems."

"That's because you're one of the most testosterone-filled men I've ever met."

"Met a lot of testosterone-filled men, have you?"

"Every day at work. Aw, fuck."

"Well, that's what I was thinkin'."

"I might hurt you. I don't feel like being incredibly considerate. Just banging it in and whipping it out."

"It's alright. I've told you. However you want. Oral if you prefer. Come on."

Phil pulled off the shirt and tie he'd worn that day at work and slipped out of his pants and y-fronts. He lay on the bed beside Mike.

"Are you sure. Any way?"

"Whatever helps. Whatever you want."

Phil nodded and kissed Mike hard. Teeth clashed as he drove his tongue into Mike's mouth. Tonight he didn't want the closeness and tenderness of love making. He wanted the sheer aggression of sex, and he was aggressive.

"Kneel on the bed," he said.

Mike knelt, and tensed. He clutched the pillow and tightened his sphincter. He couldn't help it; he'd never enjoyed being fucked from behind. Phil was used to dealing with resistance though. He pushed a fingertip through. Then his finger was in, and, far too soon, his thighs were on the back of Mike's and he was thrusting.

Despite himself, Mike's prick became hard, and he curled his hand around it. Physicality—it always excited him. He always responded. Then, to his surprise, Phil withdrew. Phil flopped down beside him.

"What the hell am I doing?" Phil asked. "I'm hurting you."

"It's okay," said Mike, turning over. "I understand."

"No. No. Come here."

This time, the kisses were different. Phil kissed Mike on his mouth, on his neck, on his nipples. He licked Mike's belly, caressed and licked the length of his prick, and kept playing with him 'til Mike said, "Ready." Then, with Mike's legs over his shoulders, grey-green eyes half-focused on his blue, he began to thrust again.

A shower of warm liquid spurted over Mike's chest, and seconds later, Phil emptied into him. The two men gripped each other as spasms made their bodies tremble. Then, with a huge shudder that signified that he was spent, Phil collapsed at Mike's side and gently nuzzled him.

"I'm sorry," he said, a few minutes later. "Whatever it was I was feeling before has evaporated. You've melted it away. I was worried, but I just felt... angry more than worried. Angry that Raith should be put in this position. Angry that the four of us should be involved with somebody else's mess. Angry. Angry. Angry. I took it out on you. I'm sorry."

"I know. I told you. It was okay."

Phil sat up and, reaching for a paper handkerchief, dried Mike's chest.

"I don't think I'm cut out for excitement," he said as he dabbed. "What with you two years ago, and me last year, and Raith this year... Ross's turn for the star role next. God, I hope not. I just want a quiet life."

"And you think you'll get it livin' with three men?"

"Hope springs eternal, as they say."

"Oh aye? Who's 'they'?"

"Don't know. Some idiots whose job it is to dish out platitudes."

"I've got a few platitudes of me own."

"Such as?"

"A snuggle a day doesn't keep the doctor away."

"Nice one."

"Early to bed and late to rise makes a man healthy, sexy and wise."

"I totally agree, although that's objectionably sexist."

"Mm."

"Also, it might be inapplicable if you're asexual."

"Asexual?"

"It could still apply, though. A person could be asexual and sexy, but not desire sex for themselves. I'll let you have that one. Another?"

"A fuck in time saves nine wanks."

"You are a really crude bugger at times. Do you know that?"

"Well what do you expect? I'm not a posh bugger like you and Ross are."

"Posh?"

"Well, you know what I mean. Backgrounds are different."

Phil was surprised. "I've never given it much thought. It doesn't bother you, does it?"

"No. I wouldn't say it bothers me. I'm aware of it. Accents, obviously, and… how would I describe it? Exposure to knowledge."

"Knowledge? You're knowledgeable. You re-built Cromarty virtually single-handed. You know the law."

"Aye, but it's a different sort of knowledge from yours and Ross's. I know about things that I need to know about. I know about the streets. I don't mean because I was a cop. I know that Bishop Auckland's not exactly a hotbed of crime, but I was always out playin', and you soon learn to deal with kids who take your ball or want to pick a fight for no reason. And I know about practical things like bike maintenance because they're the kinds of things me dad was interested in and he showed me. I don't know about theatre and art and cultural stuff. Ross knows about everythin'! Even tree fruit! He'd win *Mastermind* whereas I wouldn't get past the first round unless the questions were about vehicle stoppin' distances or the sand-cement ratio in a mix for concrete. Ross has knowledge he doesn't need, if that makes sense."

"Well, all I would say is that knowledge can be pointless, love, and dangerous. It's knowing how to use it that makes people wise. I think you're very wise. So, wise old sage, let's have another platitudinous pearl of wisdom."

Mike laughed. "Okay. A prick in the hand is worth two still inside your y-fronts."

"Hang on. You mean two different people's y-fronts?"

"Aye. Like your prick in my hand is worth Ross and Raith's pricks still in their pants."

"I wholeheartedly agree. You need to be a bit more careful with your pronouns, though."

"That's exactly what I mean! Now you're soundin' like Ross!"

"Teasing."

"Next one's yours."

And, diverted from his Raith-related worries, Phil gradually drifted asleep. Mike kissed him gently on the forehead and, not long after, slept too.

* * *

Next morning, Ross dropped Mike off in Warbridge town centre, and Mike, as planned, met Seabrooke in a café overlooking the old stone bridge that spanned the River Wear. It occurred to the sergeant that it had the feeling of a date.

"What do you think of Warbridge, then?" Mike asked as they sat down.

"Quaint compared to London," the sergeant answered.

"It's not so quaint on a Saturday night! *War*-bridge is bloody right! It can be bloody mayhem. Ask the PCs at the station."

Mike had brought the subject up. *Run with it*, Nick told himself.

"Do you miss it?" he asked.

Mike stirred his coffee more than was necessary.

"I used to," he said. "I missed the chase, but now… The guys really helped. They kept on findin' me things to do. If you'd come up here at the beginnin' of last year, all you'd have seen of me is a load of bricks. I'd have been underneath them sumwhere! Cromarty used to be just Number One, the Street, but we knocked next door through to make it bigger. That's to say, *I* knocked it through *and* did about ninety-nine per cent of the work! It kept me busy—body and mind. They're a devious little trio. It was all a sneaky little plan to get me thinkin' of sumthin' other than Warbridge bloody police station." He laughed at the memory. "And of course, it meant that Phil could move in instead of commutin' from here every night."

"I didn't realise that you'd done the bulk of the work. It's very professional. It's a really nice house."

"Don't mean to sound pedantic and stuff, but to us, it's a home not a house."

The sergeant nodded his understanding. The two men drank their coffee.

"This probably isn't the best place to talk," said Mike. "I'm takin' a bike out for a trial. If you've got an hour to kill and you fancy it, I'll take you on the back."

"What? On the back of your new bike?"

"Well, I haven't bought it yet, but why not? I'd rather talk where there aren't any other ears."

"I haven't got a helmet."

"They'll have one at the garage, and sumthin' you can wear over your jacket."

"It's a great idea. Yes."

A little later, and to his amusement and surprise, Nick Seabrooke found himself on the back of a Honda with his arms around Mike Angells' waist. He tried to analyse his feelings. More than anything, he felt... safe.

They rode through the busy, narrow town centre streets, then Mike took them out through country lanes very like the one that led to Tunhead. He weaved effortlessly round tight bends. They joined the six-eight-nine, the trunk road that led back to Warbridge, and finally stopped in a lay-by where there was a burger van.

It was only when Mike took his gloves off and started flexing his right-hand fingers that Seabrooke realised that the ride hadn't been as comfortable as he'd thought, at least not for Mike. Mike saw him looking.

"I haven't had breakfast yet," he said. "Just that coffee. Have you had anythin'?"

The sergeant nodded—he'd eaten at his lodgings.

"Do you mind if I eat while we talk?"

On being told, "Of course not," Mike bought two bacon rolls.

"I have to modify the handlebars," Mike said between bites, aware that Nick had noticed his damaged hand. "The garage did it. I could do it meself, but because this is a new bike, I'd invalidate the guarantee if I started to mess with it. It's not quite right. Needs tweakin'."

"I wouldn't have realised from the way you were riding. You're very smooth, but what else should I expect from an IAM examiner? Have you always liked bikes?"

"Aye. Me mam says I inherited three things from me dad and none of 'em were any bloody use," Mike said, grinning. "A bike, me luv of bikes and the colour of me eyes."

The sergeant resisted the urge to check out the third more closely. He didn't want to discuss paintings either. He wanted to learn about Mike.

"So, knowing, as I do, something of the way you guys deal with finance, was it easy to get the go ahead for the new bike? Did you have to plead on bended knee?"

"I had to plead on both knees and make a dozen bloody promises, includin' climbin' on the roof in a couple of weeks to put the Christmas deccies up! It's Ross's turn and he hates heights."

"Christmas decorations?"

"Oh aye. We have to have festivities. Ross and Raith insist on it. Did you notice the conifer plantation on the hill behind the quarry?"

"Ye-es."

"Well, don't tell your boss, but the owners will be a fir tree short."

"Crime of the century, heh?" said Nick, grinning. "Seriously, dealing with your families must be awkward at times like Christmas."

"In what way?" Mike asked, and took another mouthful of bacon roll.

"Well, with four of you, it doubles the 'Who do we spend the holiday with this year?' problem, doesn't it?"

"No, not really. When I was in the Force, I was usually workin' over Christmas. With not havin' children, it seemed the right thing to do. Phil's family... I've never met 'em. We're not number one on their Christmas card list. We're not on it at all, actually. Ross's family are... I suppose you could say that they're... I don't know what the word is—non-conformist, non-traditional...? His parents or his sisters might land up at our front door without any warnin', and they'd expect the same of us on theirs. It wouldn't throw them if we only had dry bread in the cupboard and fish fingers in the fridge. It takes a lot to faze them, and Ross is just the same. He's very laid back, for all he's got his finger right on the pulse of everythin'. Raith's family is the only one we might have to do some plannin' for, but he sees a lot of them through the year, and his brothers live nearer, so there's no awkwardness if he doesn't get to Lem himself—Leamington Spa—but you probably already know a lot of that already." Mike said that a little accusingly.

"I've done my homework, yes. Like you used to, though, I work over Christmas."

"Really?" Mike sounded surprised. "It doesn't seem like CID, your job."

"How do you mean?"

"Well, I don't mean to sound insultin', but it just doesn't seem as full-on as my job used to be."

"To be honest, this particular case has been somewhat exceptional. In some ways, it has seemed like a little holiday."

"Oh aye? For you, maybe. If any of my holidays involved bein' held at gunpoint in a quarry, I'd be knockin' on the door of the travel agent's and askin' for me money back."

"True, but we have our dangers too. My area is very specific and, yes, you could say that it's usually the office end of things, not the chalkface. Investigating art fraud doesn't usually involve me coming face to face with guns. It could do, though, and I've done my bit on the beat, as have all my crew. Some fraudsters are just people painting in the spare room or their garage—like Susan Osgood, for instance—but because of the money laundering link, there's always that other side of things. I don't envy the undercover guy who'll be dealing with Raith's painting."

"I'm sorry," said Mike apologetically. "I wasn't intendin' to enter the 'Who has it worst?' race. You're right. So, gettin' us back to why I'm here, and why you're here, go over it for me one more time."

A short time afterwards, Mike deposited Nick at the sergeant's lodgings. Then he returned to the garage to tell them that he'd buy the bike, but that some things needed changing. They'd have to get the bits.

Could he manage as it was for a while? He decided that, although it was awkward, he could, and rode home, as certain as he could be that Raith would be safe.

Chapter 15

A month passed, to everyone's relief, uneventfully. Raith completed the painting, and given that he and Ross had already decided to travel to London to visit a gallery that displayed Raith's ceramics, they decided to take the painting with them. The weather forecast wasn't good—there was a likelihood of snow and hold-ups on the motorway—but that wasn't a problem for people used to County Durham's vicious winter blizzards. And anyway, they'd had enough of Masha Ivashova and her tetrachromatic vision.

"Let's just get shut of the thing," said Raith. "Get it out of the way before Christmas."

The two men set off.

They'd been gone around three hours when Mike had a phone call from Amy, the tattooist.

"Hi!" said Mike. "How you doin'?"

She was fine.

"We found out about that dog I asked you about," Mike said, "but thanks for tryin' anyway."

She hadn't phoned about the dog. She'd phoned about the motto. Mike listened with increasing anxiety.

The motto was a set of six initials written in a mixture of scripts. That wasn't particularly unusual in itself. However, her tattooist friend had reason to remember doing it. The initials belonged to three men, two initials each. Shortly afterwards, one of the three had wanted to have his tattoo removed as he'd wanted to join the police. A bad skin infection had followed the laser treatment. The guy had blamed Amy's friend. He'd denied liability. Eventually the argument was settled, but it had left a nasty taste all round.

Charles King still had his tattoo.

"Amy," said Mike, "what were this other guy's initials, do you know?"

She did know: EM.

"They kicked out the wrong man!" Mike yelled to Phil.

Mike phoned Nick Seabrooke. The sergeant wasn't answering. Mike left a message. "Urgent. Call me."

"Why the panic? What's happened?" Phil asked.

"I think the guy that got suspended from the fraud crew was the wrong one. Seabrooke said he was surprised he was bent. I think the one they want is the guy who came here the first time. When they took Raith's belongings. McKeown."

Phil turned pale.

"Mike, I fucking warned you!"

"Look, I've just phoned Seabrooke and asked him to call, but maybe it's best if he doesn't. Okay, he can call the whole thing off, but if Ross and Raith get to London, they'll have to hand the paintin' over—they can't keep hold of sumthin' done with intent to deceive. And this McKeown shite will go before the police referral panel, and the scam and Raith's part in it will be one of the items discussed. And that means that—"

"I'm ahead of you. The money launderers will learn that Raith agreed to help the police go undercover."

"Phone Ross and Raith and tell them to come

home. I'll phone Flaxby. Maybe he can get a call put out to stop the Land Rover if it's spotted."

Phil phoned Raith and groaned as he heard a faint ringtone from bedroom.

"The idiot! He's left his phone here." He tried Ross instead. "Phone's off. Ross must be driving," he told Mike.

"I can't just sit here makin' phone calls," Mike said. "I'll go after them on the new bike." He began collecting what he needed. "Keep tryin' to phone Ross—they may pull in and swap drivers—and phone Flaxby. Maybe he can get Highways onto it. I'm truly sorry, Phil. You were right."

A minute later, Mike was revving up. Phil stood at the door until he was out of sight, and with the sound of the engine still in his ears, he picked up his phone and started ringing.

* * *

Further south, across the Midlands, the snow was thickening. The traffic reports were discouraging. As Phil had thought, Ross was at the wheel.

"Shall we carry on or turn back?" Ross asked Raith. "They say it won't let up."

"I dunno," said Raith. "You're driving. I suppose it's as far there as it is back, now. What do you want to do?"

"At the moment, we've got no choice: there's no turn off for a bit. Let's decide nearer the next junction."

"Fine with me."

They carried on. The traffic slowed to a crawl.

"The usual story," Raith grumbled. "First real snow and England grinds to a halt. How come they manage to keep going everywhere else?"

"I suppose England as a whole just isn't geared up for it," Ross answered. "It always seems to come as a big surprise. South of us, anyway. We know what winters are like."

"Mmm. It's getting heavier."

"I can see that! I've got the wipers on double, but they're not shifting it. We'll pull off and think what to do as soon as we can."

But by the turn off, the snow had eased off and visibility was better.

"Shall we carry on?" asked Ross.

"Might as well now we've come this far," Raith replied. "No point in going back."

* * *

Thirty miles behind them, Mike weaved his way cautiously through the first of several pile-ups. The overhead gantries were all displaying snowflakes and advising everyone to 'SLOW'. Traffic cops and ambulances used the hard shoulder, desperate to make some kind of progress. Mike was tempted to follow them, but his years in Highways told him "No!" He'd often shouted at motorway users who thought they had the right to bend the law. *"I don't care if you're late for your own funeral,"* he'd say when he caught up with them. *"You leave this lane for the emergency services. Now get back on the motorway!"*

Had Phil been able to get through to Flaxby or, better still, to Ross? He hoped so, but in case Phil hadn't, Mike knew he had to carry on.

* * *

It was just as well that he did so. Phil had phoned

the station, but Flaxby wasn't in that day. Where could he get the super's home number? Ironically, he used to have it himself. Before he moved to Tunhead, he'd sometimes stayed at the Flaxbys' when the weather was bad, but he'd erased the number from his contacts. Mike would know it, but Mike literally had his hands full.

What about BOTWAC? Ross would have Dot Flaxby's details somewhere in the BOTWAC files. Dot always attended the gallery shows, with Clive along in tow, and she'd attended several weekend activity sessions—the ones that focused on pottery. Her number would be in there somewhere.

After what seemed an age, he found it and dialled. She answered. Phil apologised for disturbing her, but he had to speak to Clive. Fortunately, she and her husband were together. Phil explained, and the super, agreeing with Phil's summation of events, promised to get the ball rolling.

* * *

Mike was struggling. Twice, he nearly dropped the bike; the tyres had no traction. Then the car he was overtaking suddenly swerved into his path. His reactions kept him upright; he had no time to think. He had problems dealing with his grip... and then, the traffic ground to a halt completely.

Mike could still manoeuvre through, of course, and—very carefully—he did so until he saw the cause of the hold up. A jack-knifed lorry blocked both lanes, and a string of cars whose drivers had misjudged their braking distance had ploughed into one another. This was the incident the cops and ambulances had been racing to.

With a mental *Sorry* to the officers present for setting such a poor example, Mike took the hard shoulder and sped through a gap between two police cars.

Half an hour later, he was sure he saw the Land Rover not too far ahead. It spurred him on. He rode alongside, matching the car's speed, and rapped on the passenger window.

"It's Mike!" Raith said, and wound the window down.

"Has Phil phoned yet?" Mike shouted.

"Don't know," Raith replied. "Why are you here?"

"Doesn't matter," yelled Mike. "Pull off next junction. It's important. Okay?"

"Okay, but what's happened?"

"Can't talk. Goin' to go under your wheels. Pull off next opp."

There were services before the junction and Ross, like many other drivers who'd had their fill of snow, signalled left and took the slip road. Mike followed. The car park was crowded, as was the restaurant. Ross queued for coffees and a bowl of soup while Raith found the three of them a table. Mike—wet, cold and tired, but relieved—phoned Phil.

"He wants to speak to you," Mike said and passed the phone to Raith.

"I'm fine!" said Raith in answer to Phil's obvious question. "We didn't know anything was wrong. Except the fucking weather. We've been listening to CDs and singing along with them."

Typical, thought Mike. Raith, blissfully unaware of danger and driving along, blithely singing, while he and Phil were going frantic... *Raith gets into trouble. Other people sort it all out for him.* It was so Raith-like, somehow.

"You look all in," said Ross as, returning, he handed Mike the soup. "Mushroom. So it says."

"I'd drink me own pee if it was hot," said Mike. "I'm frozen bloody solid."

"Phil wants to know what we'll do tonight," Raith said.

"Tell him we'll try the motel," said Ross. "If we can't get in, we'll try and find somewhere local. I don't think Mike wants to go much further."

"I'd kip on the floor right here if it was by a radiator," said Mike, gripping the soup bowl for warmth. "I'm surprised I'm not sproutin' icicles."

"We'll try the motel, and we've got spare clothes," said Ross, practical as always. "You can have a shower and a sleep. You two stay here, and I'll see what I can do."

Twenty minutes later, Ross returned with a set of room keys.

"They had a family room," he said. "A double and a single, so I took it. I've moved the car round, but you'll need to move your bike, Mike."

"Thanks. Have you got the paintin' with you, or is it still in the car?" Mike asked.

"It's here in my hold-all," said Raith. "Why?"

"Let's have it."

"What are you going to do with it?" Raith asked, watching as Ross handed Mike the canvas.

"This," said Mike. He began to gouge the paint off.

"That looks fun," said Raith. "Can I have a go?"

"Be my guest."

Raith slit the canvas with his penknife.

"I think it could do with some ketchup," said Ross, reaching for the bottle. "How's that for starters?"

The three men studied the damaged painting.

"It needs a squirt of ketchup just there, too,"

Raith suggested. He squeezed a dollop on.

"Not so much an Ivashova as an Ivash-*over*," said Ross.

"A little more texture, I think," said Raith. He tore the top off a sachet of sugar and sprinkled the contents onto the red splurge.

"The piece de resistance," Ross said, and poured the dregs of his coffee over the remains of the forged signature. "I bet they didn't have Costa Coffee where Masha lived. This painting," he announced solemnly, "is well and truly Mashared."

Shortly afterwards, they dumped their belongings on the single bed and all piled onto the king-sized double. Watching an equally king-size television, all three fell asleep, warm, fed and, in one case at least, exhausted.

* * *

Mike was still asleep next morning when Ross and Raith tiptoed down for breakfast. He joined them while they were eating, looking displeased. Ross and Raith exchanged amused glances and tried to smother smiles behind their coffee mugs.

"I can see you fuckin' grinnin'," Mike said. "I'm not bloody surprised."

"Well, you should have brought some clothes with you," said Raith accusingly. "Then you wouldn't have had to borrow ours."

"Oh really? Well next time I race half the length of England to get you out of a fix, I'll try to pack more carefully."

"You didn't fancy my things, then?" asked Ross.

"I fancied them, aye, but they didn't fancy me. I'm not used to baring my chest to strange people in motels at nine o'clock in the morning, and the trousers looked more like Bermudas. You need to grow. So, I didn't have much choice, did I?"

"That one's very nice," said Raith.

"Is it? You don't think it's just a trifle OTT, then? More suited to the Costa del Sol than to England on a winter's day? And since when have palm trees been rainbow coloured?"

"Well, I like to make a statement. You know that."

"Mm. As in 'The wearer of this shirt has the fashion sense of a field of cabbages'."

"Are you going to get some breakfast or spend the day grumbling about my clothes? Clothes that I have very generously lent you."

Mike gave Raith what Ross called his you'd-better-call-your-lawyer-you're-in-trouble look and went to the counter.

"I'm glad to see he's back to his normal sarky self," said Raith.

Ross agreed. "Me too," he said, watching Mike affectionately.

* * *

Motorway gritters had been out all night, and a single lane was clear in both directions.

An hour later, Raith and Ross continued their journey south, minus the Ivashova.

"What Ivashova?" Mike asked before he kissed them goodbye, unchained his bike and, after riding over the motorway bridge, sped in the opposite direction.

He'd spoken to Phil that morning. He knew that (a) Phil would be working 'til four, that (b) Flaxby had alerted the relevant forces as requested, but given the appalling weather, he hadn't expected a result, ("Not surprisin'," Mike had said. "It's why I felt I had to go.") and that (c) Phil had had a lengthy conversation with Seabrooke, who, it seemed, was desperate to talk to Mike. He was already aware of that; his phone was full of missed calls. He wasn't ready to talk to the sergeant just yet, however.

Home! He was so glad to open Cromarty's front door. He showered the cold away, rubbed cream into his hand and, when he could feel his fingers again, he made a brew. With a long "Phew!", he sat on the sofa to drink it.

When Phil came home, Mike was curled up asleep, a half-full mug of cold tea standing on the floor.

Phil went upstairs to fetch a travel rug to wrap round Mike. He woke him, though.

"Sorry." He ruffled Mike's hair.

Mike stretched. "Oh, hi. Shit, I feel stiff as a board. Jeezus, what a couple of days."

"You want another cuppa?" Phil indicated the half-drunk one.

"Please."

Phil made a pot and, handing Mike another mug, said, "Drink this while it's hot!" and sat on the sofa beside him. "You did well, Mike," he said, after ensuring that Mike had drunk at least half the tea. "No, you did brilliantly."

"No. Oh, I don't know, Phil. Things just seem to keep happenin', don't they? I mean, I'm not in the Force any more, but things keep happenin'. I just want a quiet life."

Phil looked at him. "Do you? I know I told you that a quiet life was what I wanted, but you? Are you sure it's what you want? I know you pretty well, Mike Angells, and the idea of you spending

the rest of your life living peacefully in Tunhead...
I can't see it somehow. Not the peacefully part.
Living in Tunhead, yes. If every farmer in the
valley lashed their tractors together and pulled,
they might manage to drag you away. You'd
dig your heels in pretty deeply though. No, you
did well. You're fierce sometimes. Frighteningly
fierce. When you're determined to do something,
there's nothing that can stop you."

"No, Phil. That's unfair. I wouldn't go against
what you and Ross and Raith decide. You know
that."

"I do know that, yes. It wasn't exactly what
I meant. I know that you abide by the quad's
decisions. I know that to my cost. You went along
with what the three of us wanted for Khaled, and
we know how that turned out. I meant that... well,
you remind me of an arrow. It's fired, and nothing
is going to interfere with its flight. It's locked onto
its target. There's no way it will miss or fail. Daniel
Bayliss last year. Charles King, and the guys in
the quarry, and riding after Raith and Ross. In
some ways, you're a very terrifying man. You
are... persistent, driven. You have to catch the
quarry."

It was true. Mike could have added another
name to Phil's list, but it was known only to
himself, to Ross, and the Flaxbys. It was linked to
his reasons for leaving the Force.

"I don't feel very terrifyin' right now," Mike
admitted.

"Well, that's your problem, isn't it? Or your
attraction. You're a man of many parts."

"Cheers. You mean I'm as bloody confused as
Raith."

"I think you are, in a way."

"Heaven help us then. As if one bloody idiot

in Tunhead isn't enough!" Mike sighed. "This had another dimension, though, didn't it? These shites were threatenin' our quad."

"Absolutely. As you said when we were up at Hartnell Force the other day: we protect the quad. More tea?"

"No, ta. I suppose I ought to speak to Nick Seabrooke. Can't be arsed at the moment. I'll do it later."

'Later' came around, and while Phil sat and chatted to Raith on one phone, Mike dialled the sergeant's number on the other.

"I don't know what to say," was Seabrooke's opener.

Mike said nothing. *You can bloody think of sumthin'. I'm not.* There was silence. Then guilt hit. After all, Mike had concurred with all the action. Despite Phil's reservations, he'd encouraged Raith to agree to Seabrooke's plan. The sergeant was only doing what a good cop should. The very thing that Phil had told Mike that he did himself: go after the baddy, whatever it takes.

"It's okay," he said. "Raith's fine. He's got his feet up in some London hotel, and he's probably running the room-service staff ragged."

"I'm really glad he's okay. Tell him so. Look, I'll word my report so that it's clear that Raith didn't wish to be involved."

"I'd rather you wrote him out of it altogether."

"I'm sure you would, but because of McKeown, it will go to an internal. I can't keep Raith's name out of it."

"I know that, but it's a case of how much you have to keep in. How far does McKeown's involvement stretch? I'm assumin' that he tipped off Amelin, the architect guy."

"Yes. Via Charles King."

"But was McKeown in contact with the gang who took Raith to the quarry?"

"Not as far as I know. At least, not directly. King seems to have been the link between McKeown and Amelin, and he hasn't been heard of for several weeks."

Mike knew why. Hopefully, King was sunning himself in the Costas, false passport in his hand. He let the sergeant continue talking.

"My guess would be that Amelin himself became scared and felt he'd be doing himself a good turn by telling the gang that Raith had tried to pass off a fake. The Susan Osgood fake, that is."

"But McKeown knows about Raith's own fake, doesn't he? The one that was on its way to London."

"Yes, of course, but if I'm right about the extent of his involvement, things have become more ugly than he ever expected, and so he's just been sitting tight. He's the problem, though, Mike. When his case goes to an internal, the full story will come out."

"No. Saying that Raith didn't want to be involved is as good as useless. This gang of shiters will hear of it and they won't see it as 'Oh, that's nice.' They'll see it as a man who was willin' to fake a picture to help get an undercover cop inside their ranks. Whether Raith wanted to get involved or not would be irrelevant. Alter your report, Nick."

"What?!"

"You heard what I said. Raith tried to help you. You have to return the favour. If you mention Raith's fake Ivashova, we'll deny any knowledge of it. There *isn't* a paintin', Nick. We'll, all four of us, say that there never was one."

There was a silence.

"What happened to it?"

"It's in three different litter bins somewhere in Leicestershire. Destroyin' it was very therapeutic."

There was another silence.

"What if McKeown himself brings it up?"

"You say, 'What's he on about?' and so do we. He won't want to say any more than he needs to, believe me. I've been up before one of these things. You say as little as you have to."

"There are other people who know: Bryn Baker, my own boss, the undercover guy…"

"No dates were set for any handover. Raith was intendin' to see you yesterday because he and Ross were comin' to London anyway. There's nuthin' official in anybody's diaries. Who cares if your Bryn Baker and one or two people ask a question or two? Say it was just an idea and nuthin' came of it. Let it just fizzle out. Same with the guy who was goin' undercover. Nick, please!"

Another silence.

"You promised that Raith would be safe. I promised him he'd be safe as well, but because one of your crew is bent, Raith's still in danger. If you knew how much we love and care for each other, the four of us, you'd understand why I'm askin' you to do a cover-up. Please, just drop it!"

"I hear what you're saying. I'll get back to you."

"Okay."

The sergeant rang off.

Nick heard what he was saying, all right, but it fell on deaf ears. Why the hell did people think that everyone in the world responded to appeals about love? Presumably because they thought that everybody's been there, done that and can't wait to do it again. Been besotted with a person. Thought about them night and day, and—as love, in most people's minds, was synonymous with sex—kissed them and touched them and done all the intimate things that he had never done and had never wished to do.

Maybe a gay man who had his choice of three others couldn't possibly understand that not everybody in the whole damn universe wanted to hear about love, love, love, and that not everybody wanted sex, sex, sex! *Damn you, Mike Angells*.

Mentally cursing Mike and his cohorts, the sergeant pulled on his jacket and stormed out of his flat.

He walked, and gradually calmed down.

He was near a bus stop, and he perched on the tiny little seat that London Transport offered weary travellers.

Why had Mike's appeal to love rankled so much? What was it he was feeling? In some ways, Nick wanted to be a part of what they had in Tunhead. The cosy domesticity he'd witnessed on his very first visit appealed to him. He'd felt envious, but his feelings had changed. He wanted more than friendship and a close connection.

Admit it! he told himself. *You're jealous.*

Of Raith, of Ross, of Phil. They had what he wanted. They had Mike. But *how* did he want Mike? If this was love, what kind of love was it? Romantic? Platonic? There were many types of love.

There were plenty of aces in queer platonic relationships. As he'd said to Phil: there, a person could feel safe in the knowledge that neither sex nor romance would be expected. But he knew that a QPR couldn't work for him. Not one in Tunhead, anyway.

For a start, he wouldn't be able to handle the quad's sexuality, even if he wasn't, himself, physically involved. It wouldn't necessarily embarrass or repulse him. He just wouldn't want to be—he laughed at his choice of words— exposed to it. The men didn't flaunt their sexuality, but its evidence was everywhere… in the pictures hanging on the walls, in the decorations in the garden, in the photographs displayed on shelves and bookcases, and most of all, in their easy-going body language. They were used to each other. They knew each other's bodies, if not through sex (he thought of Ross's 'abstinence') then through the familiarity that life together brings: bumping into each other to and from the bathroom, wandering round half-naked on hot summer days, kissing goodbye and goodnight. Even if he could come to terms with life as lived in Tunhead, what could he offer the quad in return? Nothing that wasn't there, in spades, already. They had it all. They were complete. They didn't *need* him, romantically, platonically or any other sort of "ically".

Slowly, he walked back home.

That night, he thought about Mike's request. He'd never falsified a report in his life. Was 'falsify' the proper word, though? Not mentioning Raith's fake was hardly the same as lying about it.

No—it ought to be included. It formed part of the investigation. As he'd said to Mike earlier, if it cropped up at McKeown's internal, how could its omission be explained? Could he justify leaving it out?

He didn't want to think that feelings for Mike might influence his actions. If—*if*—he ignored Raith's involvement, it would have to be for non-Mike-related reasons: common sense, gratitude and, primarily, Raith's safety. He might be jealous of Raith, but that didn't mean that he wished him any harm!

He sat down at his desk, switched on his PC and started to write.

Chapter 16

Christmas came, went, and a new year started.

Ross got up one morning and declared, "I've just had a very strange text."

"Oh, Lord, not another one," said Mike. "I was hopin' this year would be trouble free. You know what happened last time you came downstairs and started the mornin' like that."

"This was from somebody in Argentina."

"Argentina?"

"Argentina."

"Who do we know in Argentina?" asked Phil. "Maradona's not a friend of yours, is he?"

"No, and neither is this guy, but I have heard of him. His name's Basualdo. He's authored a couple of good art crits. He writes for magazines. I think he lectures. His reputation's sound."

"So…?"

"So he's asked me to phone him, and I don't know why, except that he says, in his text, that he knew Danik Amelin."

Phil and Mike exchanged looks.

"Oops," said Raith.

"You don't have to call him, Ross," said Phil.

"I'll think about it," Ross replied, and got ready to go to the gallery.

That evening, he was able to offer much more information. Carlos Basualdo had called him. "The background to this," Ross explained, "is that during and following the Second World War, a lot of people headed to Argentina. That's general knowledge. Some of the later ones were Nazis. Some of the earlier ones were, for example, German Jews, Polish Jews, Russian Jews desperate to get out of Europe. If they could take their valuables or mementos, they did so, and sometimes, that included canvases. So, there are a fair few desirable works of art lying around in Argentina. Basualdo has sometimes been able to ferret them out, and where possible, the works have been returned to the families of the original owners. Sometimes, he's bought them himself. He says that he's only done that when ownership can't be established. I can't argue with that, obviously. It's what he says. To cut a long story short, he's one of the people who provided Danik Amelin with Russian artworks. He provided an Ivashova."

"One of the Ivashovas that Amelin sold on to the money launderers?"

"I don't know. I just let him talk on. He's not stupid. He's saying that he sold paintings to Amelin. End of his involvement."

"So why has he contacted you?" asked Mike.

"Because he contacted Amelin some weeks ago over a work by another Russian painter, but Amelin explained that he couldn't make a deal because he had Raith's kidnapping case hanging over him. Basualdo knows of Raith, of course, and he knows that I'm Raith's agent and that I have a gallery. He knows I buy and sell. He's recently unearthed another Ivashova. He wondered if I'd like to buy it. That's why he phoned."

"Wow! Is he certain it's not fake?"

"Absolutely."

"Why doesn't he sell it himself?" asked Phil.

"Why go through a middle man?"

"My guess would be that he's happy to sell to respectable people, safe in the knowledge that what happens next is none of his business."

"You're respectable," said Raith, "but it's not how I'd describe the shite who kidnapped me."

"In a sense, he was respectable, Raith. He was a known art lover. He ran a respected company. He had legitimate reasons for wanting a collection."

"I suppose so," Raith admitted grudgingly.

"So this Basualdo gets a steady income, but he doesn't get his fingers dirty," said Mike.

"Precisely, and I imagine it's a bit like being a detective."

"What is?"

"Well, you used to chase people. He chases paintings. It's detective work in a way."

"Thank you very much."

"You know what I mean."

Mike said, "Mmm," without much conviction.

"Also, he knew that Amelin is dead. I'm not sure, but I wonder if he feels he'd just like to get rid of the Ivashova as quickly as possible."

"So he says, 'Which fool can I offload it onto? I know! Balan's agent, Ross Whitburn-Howe.' You haven't said yes, have you, Ross?"

"No."

"Good. Then don't."

"Phil!"

"For Christ's sake, Ross! Haven't we had enough trouble? When are we going to draw a line under this?" Understandably, Phil was agitated.

"I haven't given him an answer, because I felt we ought to discuss it first."

"Well I've just discussed it. My answer's no."

"Mike?"

Mike said nothing.

"Oh, hell," said Raith. "I recognise that look. What is it? What very important fact have we forgotten? He's doing his 'There's sumthin' you haven't thought of' thing." He mimicked Mike quite well.

"If you bought it—" Mike said.

"Mike!"

"No, Phil. Just listen. If you bought it, how much would it cost, and what would it sell for? On the open market, that is, with named buyers. No messin' around with under-the-counter private sales."

"He wants the equivalent of fifty grand in American dollars. I don't know what it would sell for. Given the current interest, three times that... four, maybe."

"What's fifty grand in our money?"

"Around forty thousand pounds. A bit under."

"Could we do it without breakin' the bank?"

"Yes."

"Fucking hell!"

"Phil, listen. Don't you remember what you read about this lady's village? It was destroyed, wiped off the map completely, and nearly everyone in it was herded up like cattle and slaughtered. Includin' her. That's total shite." Mike turned his attention back to Ross. "If you're sellin' stuff, Ross, can you insist that the buyer must be willin' to put the work on public display? No hidin' it away in a private showroom? A sort of caveat?"

"I think so. Why?"

"Then I think we ought to buy it and insist that whoever buys it off us donates it to a gallery like that one in Moscow or the one in St Petersburg that Susan Osgood visited, or even the Tate. God knows, there are enough rich Russians in London who might be willin' to dig into their pockets. Basically, I think that it's only right that this lady's work should be seen and the countryside she painted in remembered. Well?"

Mike looked at each of them in turn.

"I think it's a great idea," said Ross. "We could really capitalise on it."

"Oh aye? I can see those little money wheels turnin' in your head. That wasn't exactly why I suggested it, but we couldn't do anythin' if it weren't for the fact that you're so business-savvy, so I'll let you off. Raith?"

"Yes."

"Phil?"

"I think it's a wonderful idea," he said quietly. "Well done, Mike. What's the time in Argentina?"

* * *

"So are you flyin' to Buenos Aires to collect the picture or is this guy comin' here?" asked Mike when Raith and Phil had turned in for the night.

"Well, I was thinking of neither," said Ross.

"Oh?"

"I'm thinking of suggesting that Raith and Phil reap the benefits of Raith's recent publicity. There's a three-year waiting list for his ceramics, so our bank balance is looking very healthy."

"Don't tell him that, for pity's sake. We'd never hear the last of how he was keepin' the four of us off the breadline."

"I know! I was thinking that, if Phil could wangle it, perhaps the two of them could go, and they could throw in a visit to the Iguazu Falls."

"The ones between Brazil and Argentina?"

"Yes. I mean, they missed out on their trip to

the Angel Falls. Raith would love it, I'm sure."

"That's a grand idea, Ross. And I thought your head was full of pound signs."

"Well, it would be self-funded in a way, but we don't have to tell Raith that." Ross laughed.

"I presume we'll keep the profits on the Ivashova? That is, your new-found generosity doesn't stretch to donatin' them sumwhere?"

"I think we'd keep them. My world's full of fashions. Raith's a money-box at the moment, and has been for some time, and I hope he will continue to be one, but you never know. A bit in reserve is a good thing."

"And I don't exactly pay my way, do I?"

"That wasn't what I meant, and well you know it! If it wasn't for you, we mightn't even have Raith, so less of it!" He kissed the tip of Mike's nose. "I can't imagine that he'll still be creating erotic clay versions of you when you're old and decrepit, that's all."

"Old and decrepit, heh? I've still got a few good years in me, I'll have you know."

"Have you now? Prove it!"

"Prove it? Okay... Come on, you! Race you up the stairs!"

Cosily snuggled up to Phil, Raith heard Ross and Mike running across the landing. "What are those two squealing about?"

"No idea," said Phil sleepily. "Sounds far too energetic for this time of night."

"Mm. Night night."

"Night, love."

In their bedroom, Mike and Ross began undressing.

"Just stand there," said Mike. "I love lookin' at you. Course, I might not want to when you're old and decrepit, but you'll do very nicely for now."

Ross met Mike's gaze.

"Ah, you're givin' me that little 'Come on' look."

"I thought that was what you wanted me to do," Ross said provocatively.

"I do."

Mike placed his arms round Ross and eased him towards the bed. They stood, pressed against each other, gently grinding bodies. Fingers shaking, Mike took Ross's head in his hands and began to kiss him softly, then more fiercely.

Under the force of Mike's tongue in his mouth, Ross sank onto the bed and sighed. He loved Phil. He loved Raith. But Mike was the only one that he loved like this.

* * *

Several hundred miles away in his bachelor flat in Marylebone, Nick Seabrooke was also thinking about Mike. He'd been trying not to—with pleasing success—but Ezra McKeown's appearance before the police investigative panel was set for the following week, and Tunhead was back in his thoughts. He recalled his last conversation with the Tunhead Four, as Bryn Baker referred to the quad. The term made them sound like a cross between a boy band and a gang of terrorists.

"Well, have a good Christmas, then," Mike had said. It had sounded very final.

Nick's Christmas had been good, if good equates with pleasant, uneventful and the same as every other Christmas of the past ten years. In other words, as he'd told Phil he would, he'd spent it at work. Then, when those with family commitments had returned to duty, he'd driven down to his parents' bungalow on the Kent coast for a couple of days. Their Christmas tree had still been up, of course—an artificial one dragged out of the attic to please the visiting grandchildren. Not a patch on the one they'd have in Tunhead. What sort of decoration might the Four choose for a twenty-foot conifer? Maybe something like the 'fruit' on the 'trees' in Cromarty's garden.

He'd walked along the prom and, munching a bag of chips abstractedly, he'd stared at the grey horizon and considered the state of his life.

You're a detective, so detect! he'd told himself. *What do you know? What facts do you have?*

He'd begun to list them:

One—I do not experience sexual attraction.

Clarify your statement. What do you mean by sexual attraction?

I do not wish to participate in intimate activities with another human being. Nor an animal!

Intimate activities?

I do not want to stick my tongue in anyone's mouth. I do not want anyone to stick their tongue in my mouth. I don't want to wank anyone off. I don't want anyone to wank me off. I don't want to fuck. I don't want to be penetrated by a fingertip, let alone a penis. I have not yet met anyone who makes me want to indulge in any of the above activities. The evidence indicates that I do not experience sexual attraction.

Two—this is not a choice, it is the way I am.

Three—there is nothing wrong with my libido.

Can you clarify?

Yes, I flaming can. I'm happy to look at porn. I've studied art, for goodness sake. It's full of porn. Soft porn. Hard porn. I have no problem with porn. I get erections. I masturbate.

Ah, and when you masturbate, do you fantasise about other men?

You're hoping I'll say I fantasise about Mike Angells, aren't you? Well you're wrong.

Okay, okay, so—four—what physical activities could you indulge in?

I could sit next to someone with his arm around me, or mine around him. I could hold his hand.

Always him? Never her or them?

It wouldn't bother me if he began life as something different, but he'd have to be male now.

And what would this person be like?

My idea of good looking, smart—astute, that is, not well-dressed—thoughtful, capable of deep feelings. He'd have to be interesting, multi-layered. That's the detective in me; I'd want to uncover the truth about him. Get beneath the skin and see what's on the inside. I could get really attached to a man like that.

Isn't what you're describing just a friend? A special friend, but just a friend, nonetheless?

No. He'd be far more than a friend. There would be some physical contact. I would touch him, and hug him, and I would even kiss him lightly—but it just wouldn't be sexual, if that makes sense, and it would be more than friendship. It would be because I really liked the guy and I wanted to spend time with him and get to know him better and more closely. I would have an emotional connection. It might lead to something more, given time, but it wouldn't be that thing originally.

Well, case solved, Nick. You're a lot more ro and a lot less aro than you thought you were. You're a homoromantic asexual.

Piss off! I don't need another fucking label. And I don't feel gay.

"Get over it, you stupid twat!" he said aloud.

A passing couple briefly stared at him. His chips had gone cold. He threw them to the waiting seagulls and, annoyed with himself for wanting something he knew he couldn't have, walked back to his parents' bungalow.

Now, a month later, he was getting over it, but—clearly—he wasn't quite there yet. He groped for the switch on the bedside lamp, turned the light off and snuggled down.

"There's no reason to see any of them ever again," he told himself.

And, having assured himself that absence wouldn't make the heart grow fonder, he fell asleep.

* * *

The deals were done, and the four men sat looking at their very own genuine Ivashova. It had been too good an opportunity for Ross to miss. He decided that, rather than sell through a London house, he would hold the auction at his Gateshead gallery and employ a local auctioneer friend to work the gavel.

"Just think of the publicity!" said Ross.

"Just think of the security!" said Mike.

"Well, I'll do a Sergeant Seabrooke and sleep with the painting under the pillow," said Ross.

"You bloody won't!" said Mike. "We'll sort out sumthin' extra."

It was déjà vu—Mike advising Ross how to safeguard exhibits in a gallery.

"It's how we met," Ross said, nostalgically. "Thank heavens for thieves, heh?"

"And CID sergeants," Mike added, giving him a hug. "That's what I was, wasn't I? That reminds me, are we goin' to invite Sergeant Seabrooke to the big day?"

"What do you think?"

"I don't really see the need to. See what the others say."

There didn't seem to be much enthusiasm for doing so:

"Why?" asked Phil. "He's only interested in fakes."

"Don't see the point," said Raith. "Ask him if you want."

He wasn't invited.

He did have another opportunity to visit the little hamlet in the hills, however, and another chance to see the quad at work.

Chapter 17

"It's the first day of spring," announced a *BBC North East* newsreader gaily.

"Not here it isn't," moaned Raith as rain battered Cromarty's windows.

"No, but winter is officially over, and so are all our paint-related problems," said Phil with a sigh of relief. "Back to normal."

"Which, for us, is queer," said Raith. "That's weird, isn't it?"

Mike ignored Raith's remark. He looked at Phil and said nothing.

Ross looked at Mike and said nothing, until Raith and Phil were out of earshot.

"Okay… what was that look for?"

"What look was that?"

"The look you gave Phil when he said that all our problems were over."

"You read minds, do you?"

"Only yours. Well?"

"Well, out there…" He waved an arm at the window. "…there's a man who ordered three other men to abduct Raith and who, possibly, arranged for Danik Amelin's so-called suicide."

"I've no sympathy for Amelin."

"Neither have I, but that's not the point."

"What is the point?"

Mike took a folded postcard out of his back pocket.

"This came in yesterday's post. I've literally been sittin' on it for hours."

Ross looked at a postcard of Malaga and the two words: *James Lennard*.

"From Charles King?"

"Possibly. Publicity's a two-edged sword, Ross. He obviously worked out who I was, and perhaps he feels he owes me a favour."

"Do you call sending you this a favour?"

"Depends on how you look at it."

"It might be a trap."

"It might."

"My advice would be to tear it up and throw the pieces in the compost bin."

"I've no doubt that would be Phil's advice too. But."

"But?"

"But I like to see loose ends tied up."

"If this is a trap, you'll get tied up. Then what?"

Phil came back in.

"I'm off," he said. "Do you two want anything from Warbridge?"

They didn't. The three men exchanged goodbye hugs, and Phil drove to the hospital.

"We'll talk about it tonight, heh?" Mike suggested.

"Mike, I really think that you should just bin it. Ignore it."

"I can't. Tonight."

* * *

"No! No! And a hundred times no!" said Phil. "This isn't how it's supposed to be. We're just four guys who want to live our lives in a way we feel is right for us, and things keep bloody happening! I'm fucking fed up of it. Really. Enough."

"What about you, Raith?" asked Ross.

"I don't want us to get involved."

"That's how I felt when Mike told me about it this morning," Ross admitted. "I've had time to think about it since. More calmly. I understand what Mike means. It could be an opportunity to put a truly evil person behind bars, but I don't really want us to get involved. Perhaps we should contact Nick Seabrooke and toss it in his lap."

"And how would we explain that the postcard was addressed to Mike?" Phil asked antagonistically. "Why didn't the sender just phone Crimestoppers or something?"

"I don't see that we'd need to explain it," Ross argued. "Not given the recent publicity."

"Maybe, but Seabrooke's remit is fraud. He's not directly involved with anything else, is he?"

"But departments can't be that compartmentalised, can they? Mike?"

"They could be. I dunno. It's not a bad idea, though. It would keep us out of the firin' line. Though it all depends on what they're shootin' with."

"Great," said Phil sarcastically. There was a lengthy silence, which he broke himself. "I don't like it one little bit, but I'm willing to go along with turning it over to Seabrooke," he said unenthusiastically. "What about you, love?"

"It's okay if the sergeant deals with it," said Raith. "As long as we don't have to."

"My idea," said Ross.

"I'll phone him tomorrow, then," said Mike.

Uneasily, the four men said their goodnights.

* * *

Nick Seabrooke had mixed feelings when he

237

answered Mike's call the next day. He'd decided that he'd had a crush or a squish, nothing more, and the best way to deal with it was to focus on work and ignore it completely. It would fade, as his other 'cruishes' had faded. He'd been perfectly happy being solo before he'd met Mike. He'd be perfectly happy afterwards.

What had changed? Nothing. But, when he heard a voice with a softly spoken County Durham accent asking, "A wuz hopin' t' speak t' Sergeant Seabrooke. Izzy thur, please?" he knew that his efforts had only been partially successful. As he listened, however, professional interest overcame personal.

"And you don't know who sent the postcard?" he asked, after Mike had outlined his concerns.

"I don't know, no," Mike said truthfully.

"I'll rephrase that," said Nick. "And you have no idea who might have sent you the postcard?"

"I've no means of substantiatin' any idea I might have, so I'm not prepared to offer a suggestion," said Mike.

Cat and mouse, thought the sergeant. *I wonder which one I am.*

"I've searched online," Mike continued. "Lennard is the man behind a range of expensive developments mainly in London and in parts of Asia. I'm sure that's lucrative, but it might be a front. He's photographed with some pretty top people in some pretty top places. In the background, usually, but there."

"Such as?"

"Monte Carlo, Caribbean islands, fancy dos on fancy yachts, fishin' trips with VIPs… I just wonder what his real angle is. You'll be able to dig up a lot more than me, obviously.

"There's another thing. Ross made a list of

projects undertaken by Danik Amelin's firm. I checked it against Lennard's most recent developments. Amelin was responsible for designin' at least five of them. Maybe more. You could check. The point is, they knew each other."

"Wow. He's not Russian, though."

"No. He doesn't have to be, does he? Amelin bought Russian stuff because he was nostalgic or sumthin'. This guy might just be off-loadin' cash. If he's into money launderin', of course. He doesn't even have to like art, although I think he does."

"Why do you say that?"

"Because I checked out every shot I could find of him, and a few were taken in his very fancy office in London. I'll email a couple of 'em to you. Ross reckons you'll find 'em interestin'. The pictures hangin' on the walls, that is."

Nick was quiet. Then he said, "You are an enormous loss to CID. Do you know that?"

It was Mike's turn to be quiet. "Well, I had a lot of practice," he said eventually. "And, anyway, this one's sumwhat personal. Will you tell me the outcome?"

How could the sergeant say no?

"Yes. Definitely," he promised.

* * *

It really was spring in Tunhead when Nick Seabrooke turned in to the little lane that ran along the side of Tun Beck. The hedgerows were bright green with hawthorn, freshly in leaf, and bunches of primroses decorated the roadside verges. The sun shone and the sergeant's apprehension faded away.

A tanker collecting sewage blocked the

entrance to the hamlet. *No mains drainage. One of the disadvantages of living out here in the sticks.* He couldn't think of many others. He parked on the verge and walked the final hundred metres or so.

Spring meant spring cleaning in Cromarty, and today, it was Mike's turn to get the duster out. He'd taken the living room blinds down to give the windows a really good wash, and as he was hot and sweaty, he'd stripped to the waist. His back was to the road as Nick passed and glanced in. The sergeant was going to rap on the glass but stopped himself just in time and ducked back. Both shocked and fascinated, he wanted to look again.

Mike's back was streaked with long white lines. Vicious-looking scars. So was that what had happened when Mike had left the Force? Part of what had happened, anyway? How that whipping must have hurt! The pain must have been excruciating. His hand, his back... What the hell had occurred?

The tanker was moving up the Street. Rather than continue walking and perhaps let Mike know that he'd been spotted, Nick returned to his car and, with more revs than was necessary, drove past Cromarty to park outside Raith's studio. The stratagem worked. Mike, wearing a T-shirt, opened the door before the sergeant knocked.

He smiled and said, "Come in!"

They went into the kitchen.

"The others are all out," Mike said as he filled the kettle.

"Raith too?" asked Nick. "I didn't see his car."

"Aye. First Wednesday of the month he goes over to Consett for materials. He's got a lot of work on at the moment. Not that it seems like work to me. *This* is bloody work!" He held up a box full of cleaning materials.

"Am I holding you up?"

"I'll ask for a hand if I think you are! Might stand a chance of gettin' through the list of bloody jobs if the two of us are tacklin' the fuckin' thing."

It occurred to Nick that he liked being referred to as one half of 'the two of us'.

"I'll help if you want," he offered.

"No. I was jokin'."

Nor. A wuz jorkin'.

Nice. I've been in his presence five minutes, Nick thought, *and I'm getting sucked in again.*

"Anyway, you haven't come all this way to help with the spring cleanin'. You texted that you'd got some news?"

"Yes. I felt it was inappropriate to text you the details, or even phone. Given your input, it seemed too impersonal."

"Milk and half a spoon of sugar, wasn't it?"

He'd remembered!

Mike placed two mugs of tea on the table, and a plate of misshapen biscuits.

"Raith's," he said. "He's better with clay. They're not bad, actually, and at least he sprinkled them with cinnamon not chilli powder."

"Chilli powder? On biscuits?"

"It's a long story." Mike laughed. Then he dispensed with the informalities and said, "Well?"

"Okay. Firstly, what did you hope to achieve when you passed on the information? An arrest?"

"God, no. The CPS would have laughed at you if that's all that you'd taken them. You'd wanted someone on the inside, though. That's why you wanted Raith to fake an Ivashova. Draw these shites out of the woodwork cos you had no idea who they were. Then get your man, or woman, inside the set up."

Seabrooke nodded.

"Well you can bypass that step, can't you? We've given you a name. At least, we think we have. So you could make a connection. Get inside."

"That's what I thought you intended. That's what we've done."

"Oh?"

"Not my crew—what's left of it. I turned it over to colleagues in the National Crime Agency, and they followed your lead up. You were right in every way. Lennard knows some very interesting people. They're putting a guy into his organisation who they're sure can get closer to him. Fast boats, artworks—shares his interests. They can now watch him closely and, of course, start listing his more unusual contacts. It spreads the net. Opens the door to further investigation. Worldwide, not just here. That's what the NCA wanted. It'll take time, you know that. If it's weeks or months, that's fine. Sooner or later, there has to be pay-off. You know that too. If it's too long, he'll be a name on the records, but they'll have to drop an active interest."

It was Mike's turn to nod.

"You appreciate that Raith's abduction, the quarry one, will remain an unsolved case?"

"Aye, I know. It's TTW's anyway, not yours, and I know there's nuthin' they can do. The three guys they collared 'll keep their mouths tight shut. Short of gettin' meself sent down and beatin' the shit out of 'em in the washrooms, there's nuthin' I can do either. I'm okay with that. I know you can't get 'em all. Anyway, they're not the big guys. With a bit of luck, your undercover cop will lead you to some bigger fish."

"I hope so, too."

Nick stretched the social chit chat out as far as he could, but he rightly interpreted Mike's offer of another drink as a hint to go. Then they heard Raith's car.

"I'll be makin' him a drink," Mike said. "You're welcome to another."

The sergeant took advantage of the opportunity to stay.

"Mike, can you help me with this stuff? Oh, hello! Ooh, tea. Ta. It's great out. Really sunny and spring-like," was Raith's greeting.

"I wouldn't know about outside," said Mike drily. "I've been stuck inside, cleanin'."

"You'll help me shift stuff though, won't you?"

"His last slave died of boredom," Mike said to Nick. "I'll help you in a minute."

"I'm not in a hurry," said the sergeant. "If you want to get on with the housework, I'll help Raith unload his car."

"That's settled, then," said Raith. "Thanks."

An hour later, the sergeant, sweatier and dustier than when he had arrived, deposited the final sack of clay on Raith's studio floor.

"That's the lot," Raith said. "Thank you."

The studio was huge, and high.

"Like I said when you were here before, it was the storeroom for the quarry," Raith reminded him. "Before I moved into Cromarty, I used to live in it, too. There's a loo and a little kitchen. Have a look round, if you want, while I finish sorting."

"Thanks."

Mostly ceramics, as Nick expected. Paintings of waterfalls, some framed, some not. Nick, like Ross, knew talent when he saw it. He stared with admiration. Raith's use of colour was sensational, far more vibrant than Susan Osgood's 'Ivashova' had been and, on this larger scale, far more dramatic.

"I know you visited Iguazu recently," Nick said,

over his shoulder. "Have you done the falls there too?"

"No," Raith replied. "I didn't need to. I was happy, and my head didn't hurt. I only do waterfalls when my head hurts. Ross says that I'm living proof that Newton got it wrong."

"Sir Isaac Newton? The scientist?"

"Yes. Ross says that according to the second law of thermodynamics, things become increasingly chaotic. When I go to Harnell Force—that's the waterfall in most of the paintings, it's a couple of miles walk across the moors—I feel all chaotic and hot in my head, and the waterfall is even more chaotic. Yet it soothes me. Like Phil does, though not like Phil does, because he's calm not chaotic, so that's totally back to front."

"I'll have to think about that later," said Nick, smiling.

"Ross knows about all sorts of things," Raith said, and continued his sorting.

Then, suddenly, he raced across the floor. He was too late—Nick was already holding the painting. The two men looked at each other, then the portrait.

The tears on the canvas looked wet. Nick touched one. He couldn't help it.

"It's stunning," he said. "The colours… Astonishingly beautiful."

"Well, he's beautiful," said Raith simply. "I love him very much."

The sergeant stared at the painting. *Do I?* he wondered. *Do I?*

He didn't know.

"Don't say you saw it, please. It's a secret. He doesn't know I did it. We're not supposed to have secrets from each other. The infinity sign in our tattoos stands for openness and honesty—but sometimes, secrets aren't dishonest, are they?"

And what about my little secret? Is keeping that dishonest?

Nick was stood there, entranced by a painting of Mike Angells' eyes, discussing philosophy with one of his three lovers. How bizarre.

"I won't say a word. I promise."

He had the feeling that the promise referred to his own need for secrecy more than Raith's.

A little later, Nick and Raith returned to Cromarty.

"We've food for five," Mike assured the sergeant. "I know! I'm on cookin' as well as on cleanin' today!"

"That's kind of you," said Nick. "I'm good at peeling spuds."

"Oh aye? I'm not turnin' down a good offer. You're stayin'!" Mike laughed.

So he stayed, for what felt like the final time with this little family.

"I'd help with the washing up," he said as he drank a cup of coffee, "but I'll have to get back now."

"I'm sure Alice would put you up," Ross said.

"No—I'm at work tomorrow. Not 'til afternoon, though. If I drive through the night, I'll be able to catch a couple of hours before I start. Thanks though." It was true, and not an excuse, but he'd have made one up if he'd had to. It would only cause him harm to stay.

"Well, if you're ever up this way again, you know where to find us," said Ross kindly.

"Thanks."

They crowded round the door. They wished him a safe journey. He started the engine, and left.

Mike cleared the dishes, then joined the others in the living room.

Raith stood up and went to draw the curtains.

"You've done a good job spring cleaning, Mike. I can actually see through the window. Oh, no. You've missed a bit!"

"You know where the Windolene is," said Mike drily.

"It looks really nice out," Raith continued. It was. Quiet, and still. "Does anyone fancy a walk?"

"I'm game."

"Me too."

"And me."

The four men donned jackets and made their way up the Street and out onto the moors. They walked in silence for a while, each to the step of his own thoughts.

Raith spoke first. "Now that it's all over, and I'm not going to be had up for gun running and drug trafficking and money laundering—"

"Money launderin'? You don't even do clothes launderin'. Have you ever used an iron?"

"I was saying, before someone rudely interrupted me, that now that it's over, can somebody please explain tetrachra, tetrachro— that fucking thing I've got!"

"Your shout, I think, Phil."

"Thanks. I'll try. As you know, men aren't supposed to have tetrachromatic vision."

"That thing I've got."

"That thing you've got. To cut a long story short, it's thought to be connected with a mutation."

"A mutation? Is there something wrong with me?"

"No, love. We're all mutants to some extent."

"Some of us more so than others," said Mike meaningfully.

"You're just jealous of the length of my… hair," Raith retorted.

Mike laughed. Raith was big in every sense.

"The mutation is on a gene on the X chromosome. X and Y chromosomes determine your sex. Women, XX. Men, XY. So, women can get a double dose of the mutant gene. Men can only get a single dose. Double dose—tetrachromatic vision. Single dose—colour blindness."

"But I'm a man!" Raith repeated. "I mean, I *am* a man!"

"Well, that's a relief," said Mike. "Seein' I'd always thought I was gay."

"Can we get back to my being a tetra-thing, please? How have I got it if I can't have got it through the mutation? I had things like measles and mumps when I was little. Could it have come with them?"

Mike tutted disapproval.

"Well, if I'm a tetra-thing and I'm a man, it must have come from somewhere, so it's no use you getting all shirty."

"Aye. Sorry. You're right. How could he be tetra, Phil? Assumin' it didn't just float in on a sunbeam through the window."

"Piss off."

"Well," said Phil, "there are other explanations, though they're not fully understood yet. One thing is that tetrachromacy occurs in other species regardless of gender. Birds, fish... it's almost as though humans have lost a gene which was common in the past."

"You mean it's the rest of us who've mutated, not Raith?" asked Ross. "He should have gone out with the dinosaurs?"

"Don't you get in on the act, too!" Raith remonstrated. "It isn't funny. It nearly got me locked up. But is that what you mean?"

"Perhaps he just hasn't evolved as much as the rest of us have."

"Fuck you, Mike!"

"It's sort of what I mean, yes," said Phil. "I don't follow the research in any detailed way. It's a very different branch of medicine from mine."

"Medicine? Am I ill then?"

"No. Bad choice of words. It involves a different aspect of the human body."

"Well, I'm not a bird or a fish. I'm a man. Look! Man!" Raith unzipped his fly and delved in his y-fronts to prove it.

"Put it away, for God's sake!" said Mike, with mock disgust. "You'll scare the sheep."

"Why have I got it, Phil?"

"Well, I know that there can be a lot of variation in the properties of the opsin gene. That's the gene that carries the mutation. You may be at the extreme end. There's another possibility. Eyes have rods and cones. The rods govern what you can see at low light intensities. It's thought that, at low light intensities, the rod cells may actually contribute to colour vision. They'd give a small region of tetrachromacy in the colour spectrum. The greatest sensitivity would be at the blueish green wavelengths."

"And that's probably another reason why the police were focusing on you," Ross said. "You like to paint water and blues and greens. You choose to live in this dark and gloomy part of England. Even at the height of summer, light levels are hardly sunny Med."

"And you like bein' out at dusk. We often get worried about you gettin' lost on the moors because you're still out there paintin', long after all we see are shadows. You can still see. We can't. So maybe your rods are particularly sensitive."

"You all worry about me?"

"Did I say that? No! We just don't want to break our ankles searchin' for you after dark."

"Or stand in a load of sheep shit."

"And you're far too heavy to carry home. If you were out there injured, we'd just have to leave you 'til mornin'. Of course we worry, idiot! We love you."

"I see."

"Exactly. You do. We don't."

Raith laughed. "And the tetra bit?"

"Well, that refers to the cones. The cones are responsible for colour discrimination and intensity. Rods for light. Cones for colour. Most people have three sets of working cones—trichromatic vision. The mutation, or a high degree of variation in the opsin gene, can result in four working sets of cones. So it seems, anyway. Tetra is Greek for four. It's that fourth set that provides the extra discrimination and awareness. Does that explain it?"

"I think so. I've either got four cones or my rods are extra sensitive. Is that right?"

"That's about it, yes."

"And if I've got four cones, it's probably not the mutation, me being a man. It's more likely that I've got a highly varied opsin gene."

"Right."

"Well, my rods might be more sensitive than yours, but even I can't see much now. Do you think we better go back home before we're all deep in sheep shit?"

"Yes. Home."

* * *

"You said that everythin' would be all right, didn't

you?" Mike said to Ross as the two of them climbed into bed. "You were right."

"Mm. We only sorted it because we pull together. Group effort."

"Aye. Group efforts are great for sortin' things out, but bed's better with just you."

"Oh?"

"Mmm. Come here!"

* * *

"Ross said that everything would be all right, didn't he?" Raith said to Phil as they lay together. "He was right."

"I know. Four heads are better than one."

"In some ways. Not in others."

"I agree."

"Do you think the sergeant will have got home yet?"

"I doubt it. Why do you ask?"

"Just wondered. Do you think we'll ever see him again?"

"I don't know. Why should we?"

"I just... have a feeling that we haven't seen the last of him."

"Oh?"

"Something that he said when he was looking at one of my paintings, that's all."

* * *

The clocks had changed to summer time, and when the sergeant had driven off from Tunhead, there was still some daylight. There was a passing place a little way beyond the hamlet. He pulled into it, stepped out of his car and, for a while, looked back. Cromarty was hidden, but the tall roof of Raith's studio was visible, and he could see the little church standing on its rise.

In that moment of shared intimacy, when he and Raith were looking at Raith's painting, he'd learnt why Mike had moved to Tunhead, and he'd learnt the story behind the grave.

The colours in Tunhead's moorland backdrop began to change to purples and shades of grey. Nick got back in his car and looked at a photo on his smartphone, the only one he'd taken that day.

Layers. A man who could fly in the face of a loaded gun, and who bought flowers of remembrance every week. A man who wasn't scared to act alone, and who needed other men.

Nick's thumb hovered over 'Bin'.

He drove home.

Author Profile

Like Nick Seabrooke, the ace in the picture, I am asexual. I've chosen to paint a very narrow picture of asexuality in the story—there are so many types of aces that I could have filled a gallery. My type is very different from Nick's, but there are some firsthand truths peeping through the fiction.

I blog at polyallsorts.wordpress.com . There are posts about asexuality, polyamory, beer, tattoos, book covers and many other story-related items. There are photos of the Durham countryside, the setting of the stories, too.

Publisher Information

Rowanvale
Books

Rowanvale Books provides publishing services to independent authors, writers and poets all over the globe. We deliver a personal, honest and efficient service that allows authors to see their work published, while remaining in control of the process and retaining their creativity. By making publishing services available to authors in a cost-effective and ethical way, we at Rowanvale Books hope to ensure that the local, national and international community benefits from a steady stream of good quality literature.

For more information about us, our authors or our publications, please get in touch.

www.rowanvalebooks.com
info@rowanvalebooks.com